**STAR TREK: The Next Generation
First Year Sourcebook**

Writing
Blaine Pardo

Development
Sam Lewis

Editorial Staff
Editor-in-Chief
L. Ross Babcock III
Senior Editor
Donna Ippolito
Editor
Jim Musser
Editorial Assistant
C. R. Green
Research Assistant
Kent Stolt

Production Staff
Production Manager
Sam Lewis
Art Director
Dana Knutson
Cover Design
Dana Knutson
Illustration
Rob Caswell
David R. Dietrick

Some materials in this book were created expressly for STAR TREK: The Role Playing Game, and may be invalidated by later episodes of STAR TREK: The Next Generation

Published by
FASA Corporation
P. O. Box 6930
Chicago, IL 60680

This product is designed for use with **STAR TREK: The Role Playing Game**. It presumes a basic understanding of roleplaying games and an acquaintance with the *STAR TREK* universe.

The words *STAR TREK* stir images of the *Enterprise* on her epic five-year mission. They also elicit memories of the *Star Trek* motion pictures and of the return of the crewmembers and races that made the television show so enjoyable. The first season of **STAR TREK: The Next Generation** creates a new set of memories.

This book provides gaming information for playing **STAR TREK: The Role Playing Game** during the period covered by the first season of *The Next Generation*. It contains gaming statistics and rules that help players use the new material presented in the series.

FASA's initial roleplaying game and supplements provided information about a fictional universe that was not being further developed on television and so could be described completely without fear of contradicting future changes. *The Next Generation* is not that way at all. It evolves with each episode and continues to fill in the viewer's knowledge of the events between the motion pictures and the new series. *The Next Generation* TV series is a fluid and dynamic body of information and details.

Thus, there are several things that this book cannot do. It cannot fill in the details of the history leading to the time of *The Next Generation*. It also cannot "nail down" information that is still changing and growing, and therefore it cannot provide new star maps or detail ship classes that have not been shown. Finally, the second season additions in the cast and fiction have not been included in this work.

What this book does have is gaming statistics and gamemaster guidelines for a new generation of roleplaying in the *STAR TREK* milieu.

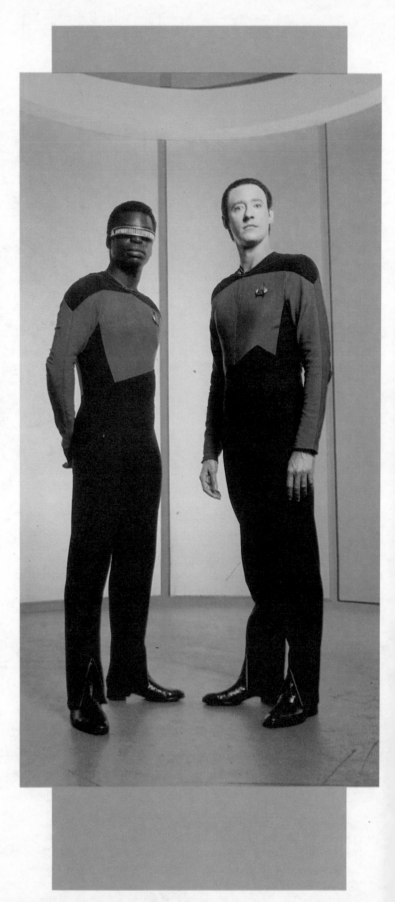

Roleplaying in *The Next Generation* has a very different feel than in the time of the original *STAR TREK*. The profound changes in the makeup and missions of Starfleet significantly alter the character of game. The new political alignment and changing universe also affect play. This section of the book helps the gamemaster adjust to this different feel.

THE NEW FEDERATION

The expansion and maturity of the Federation and its races change the character of *STAR TREK* roleplaying in several ways. The political alignments have changed, with old adversaries becoming new friends and the UFP facing new threats. All of the citizens of the Federation have their basic needs provided for, allowing them to turn their energies to activities that are fulfilling and challenging. Technological advances have pushed back the limits of known space, and Starfleet has been sent out to explore it all.

The most apparent change in the *STAR TREK* universe has been the alliance between the Federation and the Klingons. In one fell swoop, the preeminent villain in the *STAR TREK* mythos has become a trusted ally. Gamemasters shouldn't despair, though. The Klingons are still culturally a people who consider military expertise the highest of all virtues, a belief at odds with the Federation's own values. Additionally, the Klingon alliance with the Federation has generated a reasonable level of internal unrest among elements of the Klingon peoples (see the "Heart of Glory"). Both of these elements can be used as plot devices in scenarios that feature Klingons.

THE PRIME DIRECTIVE

Starfleet is dedicated to the expansion and exploration of space. To that end, the primary mission of all their starships is exploration or the support of that effort. With the Starfleet exploration effort, hundreds of first contacts began to take place. These first contacts seem to have brought stricter enforcement and interpretation of the Prime Directive. Breaking the Prime Directive is considered the most grievous violation of Starfleet regulations and is grounds for immediate dismissal.

The gamemaster should stress this fact to the players. To violate the Prime Directive is to end your career in Starfleet, plain and simple. Boards of Inquiry on Prime Directive matters should be common during *The Next Generation*, and each ship is subject to unannounced inspections by the Inspector General's Office. Such inspections often occur once every standard year, depending on the patrol station of the vessel.

The gamemaster may wish to use such inspections to keep officers honest. The Inspector General's staff would interview all pertinent personnel, review the ship's logs, and generally harass the players to admit that something is amiss aboard a ship or that they have violated some regulation (see "Coming of Age" for details). With proper timing, the gamemaster can use such inspections to make sure characters do not bend the Prime Directive.

THE PRIME DIRECTIVE

As the right of each sentient species to live in accordance with its normal cultural evolution is considered sacred, no Starfleet personnel may interfere with the healthy development of alien life and culture. Such interference includes the introduction of superior knowledge, strength, or technology to a world whose society is incapable of handling such advantages wisely. Starfleet personnel may not violate this Prime Directive, even to save their lives and/or their ship, unless they are acting to right an earlier violation or an accidental contamination of said culture. This directive takes precedence over any and all other considerations, and carries with it the highest moral obligation.

GALAXY CLASS

Improvements in warp technology have changed space travel. At its maximum speed of Warp 10 (100,000 times the speed of light), the *Enterprise* could traverse the galaxy in a year. The new USS *Enterprise* is designed for a mission that can last 15 to 20 years. This effectively opens up the galaxy to exploration, boldly facing new challenges and new races. Thus, gamemasters should no longer feel that they must restrict their scenarios to the well-known old Federation borders.

Galaxy Class ships like the *Enterprise* are innovative, both technologically and socially. On the technological side, the *Galaxy* Class ship represents the cutting edge of Federation science. Faster than any other ship in known space, the *Galaxy* Class will be at the forefront of any exploration effort in which Starfleet wishes to engage. For the gamemaster, this presents plenty of opportunity to have his players directly interact with high-echelon Starfleet officers.

Galaxy Class ships are not just the biggest and fastest ships in the fleet, but they also present the cultural and social values of the Federation in microcosm. Not only are members of Starfleet serving aboard the ship, but their families are there, too. Starfleet included families aboard the *Galaxy* to make long exploration voyages more palatable. Gamemasters can assume that Starfleet will begin this type of assignment on other vessels.

Families give a gamemaster a wealth of nonplayer characters to create another layer of motivations and interactions for the players. When the ship is threatened, an officer may react differently if his family is aboard. The whole atmosphere aboard ship is different with children present. A good gamemaster will use families to create tension among the players. Imagine the plight of an officer on the bridge about to face a potentially hostile Ferengi cruiser. Suddenly he gets an urgent message from his wife. Their precocious twelve-year-old son has just stolen and launched a shuttlecraft! Gamemasters should not overuse family difficulties, but reserve them to breathe new life into a session.

NEW THREATS

Though the Federation is at peace and in the midst of a renaissance, there are still threats that can be used in scenarios. The Ferengi Empire presents a source of future difficulties. The return of the Romulan presence in "The Neutral Zone" is another potential threat.

The Ferengi pose a number of challenges because they trade with many worlds and thus have long and strong economic tentacles. Money and greed are powerful motivators of what others might consider criminal behavior. Gamemasters will find the Ferengi helpful in introducing greed into the Federation.

There is also a new and unusual threat to the Federation in the form of an insectoid parasite that can take over humanoids. The parasite captured some of Starfleet's highest officers and would have gained control of the Federation if not for the swift action of Captain Jean-Luc Picard. Though the initial assault of this race is apparently over, there are fears that the insectoids may return to the Federation or are already there.

NEW SHIP POSITIONS

The changing emphasis of Starfleet's role and the introduction of the *Galaxy* Class have altered the functions of Bridge positions in the roleplaying game. Several positions are added, and personnel now have the training to perform a number of tasks.

Instead of individuals assigned to Helm and Navigation, the *Galaxy* Class has two Bridge Command Specialists, each trained to fill the other position. The *USS Enterprise* is the first vessel to utilize these positions. The success of this program has prompted a gradual implementation throughout the fleet.

What does this mean to the gamemaster? With Helm and Navigation responsibilities interchangeable, the Gamemaster must make sure that the Captain delegates duties. Some players may need to change the duties of their characters. Traditional roles from the original *STAR TREK* no longer exist. For example, the functions of Communications Officer are now spread among other characters on the Bridge.

Though there is potential difficulty because of overlapping functions, in the long run, it allows players to experience a range of duties on the Bridge.

BRIDGE COMMAND SPECIALIST

The Helmsman Bridge Command Specialist executes the Captain's movement orders. This person uses the *Starship Helm Operation* Skill Rating. This specialist handles ship-to-ship communications by making a die roll against the *Communication Systems Operation* Skill Rating to open hailing frequencies or establish contact with another ship or star base.

The Navigator Bridge Command Specialist uses *Astrogation* skill to predict the course of the ship for movement. The Navigator Bridge Command Specialist no longer operates the deflector shield. The Navigator does have access to a starship's long-range sensors, however, and may retrieve tactical information by making a die roll against the *Starship Sensors* Skill Rating. This can be used with the *Computer Operation* skill for loading data into the ship's computers.

ENGINEERING SYSTEMS SPECIALIST

The Engineering Systems Specialist performs the traditional functions of the Chief Engineer. Of all the duties in starship combat, this is the least changed. This character still makes skill rolls against *Warp Drive Technology* to increase power levels and against his *Astronautics* Skill Rating for superstructure repairs. The Engineering Systems Specialist executes the power-allocation orders of the Captain or the First Officer, just as in the original **STRPG.**

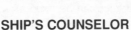

SECURITY SPECIALIST

One of the most important officers during starship combat is the Security Specialist. This person fires all starship weapons by making skill rolls against *Starship Weaponry Operation*. The Security Specialist also controls the ship's shields by rolling against his or her *Deflector Shield Operation* skill. This character doubles as the Security Officer. The Security Specialist controls starship security and internal communications. Players should roll against their *Security Procedures* and *Communications Systems Operation* skills when appropriate. Aboard the *Galaxy* Class, this officer's position is facing forward, just aft of the Captain's seat, with a full view of the Bridge. Modifications are made on older starships to accommodate similar command consoles.

MEDICAL OFFICER

This role is substantially unchanged. The Medical Officer still treats the injured by making skill rolls against *General Medicine*. The Medical Officer receives an automatic communications link with the Tactical Specialist's station on the Bridge whenever the ship is on Red or Yellow Alert. This monitoring can save critical time in preparing the ship's medical facilities for emergencies.

SCIENCE SPECIALIST

The Science Specialist has a narrower role than the original Science Officer. The Science Specialist controls sensors other than those used for combat. Making skill rolls against *Starship Sensors*, this officer determines the nature of lifeforms or beings and relays environmental data to the Tactical Specialist. This role is limited in combat, but it is crucial during first contacts. The Science Officer also relays information about the Bridge crew's psychological state to the Medical Officer.

SHIP'S COUNSELOR

The introduction of the Betazoid race into the Federation and the subsequent creation of the position of Ship's Counselor create a number of problems or opportunities for the gamemaster. Betazoids and even beings with strong Betazoid ancestry can read emotions, feelings, and body language. Through empathy, they can determine a great deal about new races. This is the reason for creating the position of Ship's Counselor, so a Betazoid can advise the captain about a new race.

Telepathic among their own race, Betazoids are only empathic with other lifeforms. Thus, Betazoid characters are only able to *interpret* the thoughts and emotions of other lifeforms. Even this ability is not infallible or unlimited. Conflicting emotions and feelings can confuse the Betazoids or give them a false reading. This is very similar to what happens when a person walks past people in conversation and catches only a portion of what was said. The range at which Betazoids can detect feelings and emotions is also variable. These restrictions give the gamemaster great latitude in feeding information to the players and guiding players through an adventure. By placing a random thought from a nonplayer character in a Betazoid's mind, a gamemaster can lead players to stunning successes. Likewise, a good gamemaster can also use these characters as a tool to mislead players.

TYPICAL MISSIONS

As a guide to the gamemaster, listed below are some of the typical missions that can be used as a basis for *Next Generation* scenarios. Note that many scenarios can include elements of two or more missions.

Exploration
Transporting Important Passengers
Diplomatic and Trade Missions
Patrolling Disputed Boundaries
Mediation and Negotiation
Responding to Ships in Distress
Routine Vists to Planets/Colonies/Space Station
Scientific Missions
Defensive Actions Against Threats to Federation
    Planets
Military Maneuvers
Testing New Equipment
Training Missions
Police/Security Force Where Requested
Showing the Flag
Crisis Control
Terrorist/Hostage Rescue

Gamemasters might wish to incorporate the crewmembers of the new *Enterprise* into their campaigns as either player or nonplayer characters. Using these characters as nonplayer characters helps the gamemaster in many ways. Both the gamemaster and the players are familiar with the characters, and so there is no need for detailed explanations of the character's behavior. Because everyone knows that Dr. Beverly Crusher is Wesley's mother, her desire to violate, or at best, bend, the Prime Directive to save him is understandable. Conversely, having a well-known person behave out of character can be used as a signal to the players that something is amiss. Having Captain Jean-Luc Picard lead an Away Team, and having First Officer William Riker acquiesce without protest should send all the players scrambling for an explanation.

Another advantage to using these characters instead of generating new ones is that each player immediately knows his character's personality. Data is basically a competent Pinocchio who wants to be human. Worf is constantly struggling between his Klingon instincts and his Federation training. La Forge has accepted his blindness, but there are times when a desire to see normally can hit him hard, as in "The Naked Now." A player will know how his character reacts and interacts with the other members of the crew. Picard and Riker have a very close relationship. Each knows what the other expects of him in any given circumstance. Wesley worships Riker. With these characters, players can immediately begin to play their roles to the fullest extent.

Name: PICARD, Jean-Luc
Rank/Title: Captain
Position: Commander, *USS Enterprise*

Race: Human
Age: 54
Sex: Male

Attributes:

STR	60	CHAR	62
INT	78	LUC	40
END	68	PSI	15
DEX	70		

Combat Statistics:
To-Hit Numbers–   Bare Hand Damage: 1D10+3
  Modern: 50   AP: 11
  HTH: 57

Significant Skills	Rating
Administration	44
Computer Operation	42
Computer Technology	34
General Medicine, Human	15
Holodeck Operations Procedure	31
Language	
French	88
Klingonaase	30
Leadership	81
Marksmanship, Modern	30
Navigation, Helm	40
Negotiations/Diplomacy	83
Personal Combat	
Armed	65
Unarmed	64
Planetary Survival	23
Psychology, Human	40
Security Procedures	49
Shuttlecraft Pilot	40
Shuttlecraft Systems Technology	20
Small Unit Tactics	56
Social Sciences	
Federation Culture/History	41
Federation Law	33
Sports	
Fencing	35
Starship Helm Operation	27
Starship Combat Strategy/Tactics	70
Trivia	
Earth History, France	50
Earth Mystery Novels	60
Warp Drive Technology	55

Distinguishing Physical Characteristics:
Though only of average height, Captain Picard gives the impression of being tall and imposing. His most striking characteristic is that he is balding. He is in excellent physical condition and very athletic. Captain Picard has a stern, commanding voice that demands attention.

Brief Personal History:
Born in Paris, France, Jean-Luc Picard failed his first entry exam into the Academy. Despite this inauspicious beginning, Picard rapidly rose through the ranks and was assigned as Captain to the *USS Stargazer* while still in his early thirties. Under his command, the name *Stargazer* became synonymous with space exploration and travel after an incredible 22-year mission.

His greatest regret during his command of the *Stargazer* was the loss of his best friend, Jack Crusher. Crusher was killed on an Away Team mission, and Picard returned the body to his widow, Beverly Crusher, for burial. Picard took years to recover from the loss, though he gained a heightened appreciation for the value of each member of an Away Team.

The ship ended its long career when it encountered an unknown vessel that turned out to be one of the Federation's first meetings with the Ferengi. With his ship crippled, Captain Picard ordered the *Stargazer* into a micro-second warp just as the pirate was preparing to fire. For a split-second, the ship appeared to be in two places at the same time, throwing off the enemy attack. Picard fired at the pirate at point-blank range, destroying it. Though he had to abandon the *Stargazer*, he and his crew survived and were able to report the encounter to Starfleet. Captain Picard's micro-second warp jump is now taught in Starfleet Academy as the "Picard Maneuver."

When the *Galaxy* Class *USS Enterprise* was commissioned, he was the natural choice for its captain. Not only did he get command of the *Enterprise*, but he also received the right to pick the crew. His only hesitation in taking command of the new ship was the presence of crew members' families. Picard has always felt uncomfortable around children, but he considers this uneasiness a small price to pay for the command of such a ship.

Captain Picard has turned down several promotion opportunities, including one to Commandant of Starfleet Academy, a very prestigious position. His experience with non-space commands left a bitter taste in his mouth, and he much prefers his present position.

Personality:
Jean-Luc Picard spends little time looking to his past, though he places a high value on his friendships. There is a touch of French phrasing in his speech, though his Gallic accent only comes to the forefront when deep emotions are triggered. He is a romantic, sincerely believing in concepts such as honor and duty.

Name: RIKER, William T.
Rank/Title: Commander
Position: First Officer, *USS Enterprise*

Race: Human
Age: 33
Sex: Male

Attributes:

STR	69	CHAR	72
INT	70	LUC	50
END	78	PSI	25
DEX	68		

Combat Statistics:
To-Hit Numbers–   Bare Hand Damage: 1D10+3
  Modern: 49   AP: 11
  HTH: 42

Significant Skills	Rating
Administration	79
Artistic Expression	
Jazz	32
Computer Operation	46
Computer Technology	10
Damage Control Procedures	55
Deflector Shield Operation	33
Environmental Suit Operations	20
General Medicine, Human	06
Holodeck Operations Procedure	22
Instruction	55
Language	
Klingonaase	16
Telleran	07
Leadership	68
Marksmanship, Modern	31
Navigation/Helm	30
Negotiations/Diplomacy	41
Personal Combat	
Armed	24
Unarmed	17
Security Procedures	31
Shuttlecraft Pilot	21
Small Unit Tactics	70
Social Sciences	
Betazoid Culture	18
Federation Culture/History	22
Federation Law	30
Starship Combat Strategy/Tactics	58
Starship Helm Operation	38
Starship Sensors	41
Starship Weaponry Operation	70
Transporter Operation Procedures	35
Trivia	
History, USS *Enterprise* Logs	27
Warp Drive Technology	30
Zero-G Operations	08

Distinguishing Physical Characteristics:
William T. Riker is tall and has dark hair and deep-set eyes. He is fit and spends most of his spare time learning all he can to improve his performance.

Brief Personal History:
Will Riker was born in Alaska and entered Starfleet Academy with an impressive score. His ambition and drive quickly earned him the rank of Commander and eventually an offer to command the *USS Drake*. He turned this offer down in favor of accepting the position of First Officer aboard the *Enterprise*.

As First Officer, Riker sees protecting the life of the Captain as one of his major responsibilities. This has led to the only blemish on his record. When serving as First Officer on his first ship, Riker refused to beam Captain DeSoto down to Altair IV because he felt that the situation was too dangerous. Captain DeSoto thinks highly of Commander Riker, but he did note Riker's refusal in his permanent service record.

As First Officer, Riker has the responsibility to present to the Captain with a completely functional vessel, along with a fully-trained crew. These "housekeeping functions" are not as glamorous or exciting as leading an Away Team, but Commander Riker has performed those duties in a outstanding manner.

Personality:
Commander Riker prides himself on knowing the strengths and weaknesses of the crew and Away Teams and on utilizing the right of people to solve problems.

He has a special sense of humor that has served him well in his leadership position aboard the ship. He accepts responsibility for the Away Team missions, not because he feels that he can do a better job than the Captain, but because he knows that the loss of Captain Picard would spell the end of any *Enterprise* mission.

He has an excellent relationship with Captain Picard. As a team, they complement each other well. Picard trusts Riker to ensure that the ship and crew are at a high state of readiness at all times, and Riker has a burning ambition to prove himself worthy of Picard's faith in him.

Name: CRUSHER, Beverly
Rank/Title: Commander, Doctor
Position: Chief Medical Officer, *USS Enterprise*

Race: Human
Age: 41
Sex: Female

Attributes:

STR	42	CHAR	67
INT	77	LUC	46
END	65	PSI	17
DEX	69		

Combat Statistics:
   To-Hit Numbers–   Bare Hand Damage: 1D10
      Modern: 48   AP: 10
      HTH: 34

Significant Skills	Rating
Administration	46
Computer Operation	66
Damage Control Procedures	68
Environmental Suit Operations	30
Instruction	31
Language	
Vulcan	15
Life Sciences	
Biology	17
Bionics	38
Xenobiology	70
Life Support Systems Technology	30
Marksmanship, Modern	28
Medical Sciences	
General Medicine, Human	76
General Medicine, Betazoid	14
Pathology	58
Psychology, Human	56
Surgery, Human	70
Personal Combat, Armed	20
Physical Sciences	
Chemistry	42
Physics	20
Planetary Sciences	
Hydrology	08
Social Sciences	
Federation Culture/History	25
Federation Law	30
Starship Sensors	10
Transporter Operation Procedures	30
Zero-G Operations	23

Distinguishing Physical Characteristics:
   Beverly Crusher is tall and has red hair. Her face is drawn and narrow, and she has large hands with long fingers.

Brief Personal History:
   As a young child, Beverly was drawn to the practice of medicine on the Alveta III colony where she was born. Ten years earlier, a plague nearly wiped out the planet's population. Her grandmother improvised medical treatment until a Starfleet relief vessel arrived. Beverly learned of the herbs and roots that her grandmother had used in her cures and fell deeply in love with medicine and helping others.
   While attending Starfleet Academy, Beverly met Jean-Luc Picard and his close friend, Walker Keel. The three became fast friends, and it was Keel who introduced Beverly to Jack Crusher. She and Jack fell in love, married, and had a son, Wesley. They were together for most of their careers. However, when a berth opened up on the *USS Stargazer*, Jack Crusher took the opportunity to serve with his old friend Jean-Luc Picard.
   That was the last time Beverly saw her husband. Captain Picard returned Jack's body to her, and Jack Crusher was honored as a hero of Starfleet.
   Years later, when the position of Chief Medical Officer of the new *USS Enterprise* was posted, she did not hesitate to request the assignment. Though many at her Starfleet Review Board were concerned that she might harbor bad feelings toward Captain Picard, Beverly was steadfast. She and Wesley were assigned to the new *Galaxy* Class starship. She viewed the posting as a boost for her career, a chance to be near her son, and an opportunity to bury some of her feelings about the loss of her husband.

Personality:
   Beverly Crusher is forward and direct. If she does not like something, she will say so. She often appears to be cold, especially toward males. It takes her a long time to allow herself to open up to others.
   While she understands that Captain Picard was not responsible for her husband's death, she still has not fully resolved all her feelings about the event.

Name: LAFORGE, Geordi
Rank/Title: Lieutenant J.G.
Position: Navigator, *USS Enterprise*

Race: Human
Age: 28
Sex: Male

Attributes:

STR	65	CHAR	70
INT	70	LUC	43
END	68	PSI	13
DEX	65		

Combat Statistics:
  To-Hit Numbers–   Bare Hand Damage: 1D10+3
    Modern: 45   AP: 10
    HTH: 43

Significant Skills	Rating
Administration	30
Computer Operation	40
Computer Technology	39
Communication Systems Technology	35
Damage Control Procedures	47
Deflector Shield Operation	42
Electronics Technology	48
Holodeck Operations Procedure	33
Holodeck Systems Technology	58
Instruction	14
Leadership	46
Life Support Systems Technology	31
Leadership	46
Marksmanship, Modern	25
Mechanical Engineering	52
Medical Sciences	
General Medicine, Human	12
Navigation/Helm	59
Negotiations/Diplomacy	28
Personal Combat	
Armed	24
Unarmed	17
Small Equipment Systems Operation	23
Space Sciences	
Astrogation	57
Astronautics	34
Astronomy	51
Astrophysics	23
Starship Combat Strategy/Tactics	55
Starship Sensors	50
Starship Weaponry Operation	22
Transporter Operation Procedures	18
Warp Drive Technology	50

Distinguishing Physical Characteristics:
  Geordi LaForge is short and dark-skinned. His most obvious physical characteristic is the visor he wears across his eyes. Blind due to a birth defect, Lieutenant LaForge uses this visor to "see".

Brief Personal History:
  Geordi LaForge is racially black and birth-defect blind. Because there was no formative matter in his eye sockets, doctors could not give him sight through surgery. Most people's spirits would have been crushed by this handicap, but LaForge seemed to treat it as only a minor inconvenience.

  This spirit captivated a top medical/electronics team, who developed the VISOR (Visual Instrument and Sensory Organ Replacement) for his use. This device consists of surgical implants to the vision centers of the brain as well as an external sensor/visor. It allows LaForge to "see" in a wide range of spectra better than a normal human, but it does not replace vision. Though he received the implant at an early age and has always experienced discomfort with the device, he is blind without it.

  When the *Enterprise* was commissioned, Lieutenant LaForge, then aboard the *Hood*, requested a berth on this great ship. When asked why he wanted to serve aboard her, he replied: "Who wouldn't, sir? The biggest, newest, fastest starship in the fleet…"

  Since his arrival aboard the *Enterprise*, LaForge has faced a number of challenges. He showed great leadership in his first command over the planet Minos and received a commendation from Captain Picard. He enjoys being a member of the Away Team and using his unique vision to help the landing party.

Personality:
  Laforge can be best described as a blithe spirt. His humor is sometimes flippant and irreverent, but is a capable and competent officer, as shown by his command of the *Enterprise* during the incident over Minos.

  He does not feel hindered by his handicap, but there are times he wishes that he could see normally.

  He greatly admires Captain Picard and Commander Riker as his superior officers. Though he enjoys his position as Navigator for the *Enterprise*, he hopes soon to be posted as the Ship's Engineering Officer.

Name: CRUSHER, Wesley
Rank/Title: Acting Ensign, *USS Enterprise*
Position: Bridge Specialist

Race: Human
Age: 16
Sex: Male

Attributes:

STR	41	CHAR	58
INT	87	LUC	70
END	56	PSI	20
DEX	70		

Combat Statistics:

To-Hit Numbers–   Bare Hand Damage: 1D10
  Modern: 35   AP: 11
  HTH: 35

Significant Skills	Rating
Computer Operation	50
Computer Technology	46
Electronics Technology	33
Holodeck Operations Procedure	39
Holodeck Systems Technology	41
Mechanical Engineering	66
Navigation/Helm	33
Shuttlecraft Systems Technology	20
Starship Combat Strategy/Tactics	10
Starship Helm Operation	31
Starship Sensors	12
Transporter Operation Procedures	18
Transporter Systems Technology	23
Warp Drive Technology	52

Distinguishing Physical Characteristics:

Wesley Crusher has a medium build and light brown hair. He is quite young and looks his age.

Brief Personal History:

Wesley Crusher is considered a prodigy. As the only child of Jack and Beverly Crusher, Wesley has spent his entire childhood on a variety of Starfleet installations or ships.

Wesley has very few memories of his father. His most vivid is of when Captain Picard, then the Commanding Officer of the *USS Stargazer,* returned his father's body to Terra for burial.

Wesley developed an early love of advanced engineering and physics, particularly with warp-drive intermix computations and tractor/repulsor beam technology. His fascination with these subjects and his assignment to the *Enterprise* have given him an outstanding background. Though many Starfleet engineers have great difficulty with the the maze of circuitry layouts and design patterning, Wesley can visualize such systems easily and reprogram them in his head.

Despite some earlier reservations, his mother has granted him permission to enroll at the Academy. His first application was outstanding, but he lost out to one other applicant. Commander Riker is concentrating Wesley's studies on his weak areas, history and chemistry.

Captain Picard has awarded Wesley the honorary position of Acting Ensign for his actions aboard the ship and because of a special request from an alien known as The Traveler. Captain Picard has a standing order that Wesley be treated as a full ensign. Captain Picard also put his First Officer in charge of Wesley's training and studies.

Because of his closeness with Picard and Riker and because of his honorary rank, Wesley has full access to the *Enterprise*, including the Bridge. In routine operations, he is allowed, under strict guidance, to navigate and even to take the helm occasionally. Captain Picard has begun to use Wesley as a buffer with children and other civilians, even allowing Wesley on a few Away Team missions.

Personality:

One of Wesley's difficulties with his peers is that his exceptional intelligence often overwhelms his classmates and friends. He is still quite popular and is very sociable despite his interests in studies.

Wesley feels that most adults ignore him because of his age, but in fact, he lacks experience and tact. He is sometimes belligerent and surly toward his elders. Despite his intelligence, Wesley is still a chid and is still exploring the limits of his social behavior.

Name: WORF
Rank/Title: Lieutenant
Position: Security Chief/Weapons Officer, USS Enterprise

Race: Klingon
Age: 34
Sex: Male

Attributes:

STR	80	CHAR	37
INT	72	LUC	30
END	70	PSI	09
DEX	69		

Combat Statistics:

To-Hit Numbers—   Bare Hand Damage: 2D10
    Modern: 68   AP: 10
    HTH: 74

Significant Skills	Rating
Administration	28
Computer Operation	33
Computer Technology	22
Damage Control Procedures	39
Deflector Shield Operation	40
Language	
English	80
Klingonaase	25
Leadership	50
Marksmanship, Modern	67
Negotiations/Diplomacy	14
Personal Combat	
Armed	77
Unarmed	80
Personal Weapons Technology	12
Planetary Survival	37
Psychology	
Human	22
Klingon	67
Shuttlecraft Pilot	12
Small Unit Tactics	40
Social Sciences	
Federation Culture/History	26
Federation Law	20
Klingon History	55
Sports	
Parrises Squares	44
Starship Helm Operation	20
Starship Weaponry Operation	60
Transporter Operation Procedures	34
Trivia	
Klingon Sayings	60
Warp Drive Technology	20

Distinguishing Physical Characteristics:

Worf is an average-size Imperial Klingon, though tall and muscular by human standards. He has dark brown eyes and black hair. He wears a Klingon warrior's sash on his uniform.

Brief Personal History:

Worf remembers very little about his parents or his childhood on the world of Khitomer. A Romulan raid killed everyone in the colony except him. Starfleet dispatched a ship in response to the emergency call, but it arrived far too late. A Starfleet officer found Worf and legally adopted him, sending him to live with the officer's family on the farming world of Gault.

Worf and his foster brother enlisted in Starfleet Academy, but his brother returned to Gault after the first year. Worf excelled, and became the first Klingon officer in Starfleet.

As a Bridge Weapons Officer, he acted in a number of positions during the initial mission of the *Galaxy* Class *USS Enterprise*. After the death of Security Chief Tasha Yar, he quickly stepped into her role. He considers the position a great honor despite the way he received it.

Personality:

Though he is a Starfleet officer, Worf has dedicated himself to living as a Klingon officer. He feels a great deal of stress in trying to reconcile adapting to humans on a personal level while behaving as a true Klingon.

Worf is fast in action, responding to aggression more from reflex than from calculated thought. His skills in fighting are well-known, and he is an aggressive athlete as well.

He strives to demonstrate control of a situation. Though Worf is predisposed toward violent action, he takes pride in maintaining self-control.

Name: DATA
Rank/Title: Lieutenant Commander
Position: Helmsman, *USS Enterprise*

Race: Android
Age: N/A
Sexual Appearance: Male

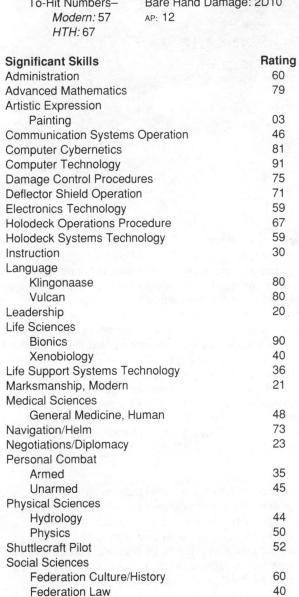

Attributes:

STR	99	CHAR	47
INT	87	LUC	05
END	99	PSI	00
DEX	89		

Combat Statistics:
  To-Hit Numbers–   Bare Hand Damage: 2D10
    Modern: 57   AP: 12
    HTH: 67

Significant Skills	Rating
Administration	60
Advanced Mathematics	79
Artistic Expression	
Painting	03
Communication Systems Operation	46
Computer Cybernetics	81
Computer Technology	91
Damage Control Procedures	75
Deflector Shield Operation	71
Electronics Technology	59
Holodeck Operations Procedure	67
Holodeck Systems Technology	59
Instruction	30
Language	
Klingonaase	80
Vulcan	80
Leadership	20
Life Sciences	
Bionics	90
Xenobiology	40
Life Support Systems Technology	36
Marksmanship, Modern	21
Medical Sciences	
General Medicine, Human	48
Navigation/Helm	73
Negotiations/Diplomacy	23
Personal Combat	
Armed	35
Unarmed	45
Physical Sciences	
Hydrology	44
Physics	50
Shuttlecraft Pilot	52
Social Sciences	
Federation Culture/History	60
Federation Law	40
Space Sciences	
Astrogation	40
Starship Helm Operation	70
Starship Sensors	70
Starship Weaponry Operation	65
Transporter Operation Procedures	47
Trivia	
General	31
Warp Drive Technology	66

*Data's characteristics are heavily weighted due to the fact that he is an android and can recall every fact and event that he experiences. Also note the Trivia (General) skill. The gamemaster should use this rating as a catch-all knowledge skill. Data has a good chance of knowing something about everything.

Distinguishing Physical Characteristics:

Commander Data appears as a human with light yellow skin and yellow eyes. He can remember everything that he learns or sees. He has an "On/Off" switch on his lower back, but few individuals know this. Commander Data can read text at amazing speeds and can digest the information as fast as any computer.

Brief Personal History:

Professor Noonian Soong had a dream of creating the perfect android with a positronic brain. Ostracized because of his failures, Professor Soong retreated to Omicron Theta to conduct his experiments. He created two such androids before a mysterious and murderous Crystal Entity attacked the science colony, leaving only the android called Data.

The *USS Tripoli* arrived at the colony to find only Data remaining. When the crew of the *Tripoli* activated Data, they found the collective memories of the colonists stored in his mind. Furthermore, Data seemed to have purpose, drive, and a strong desire to interact with human beings.

After graduating with honors from Starfleet academy, Data served on a number of Starfleet vessels and earned several honors and awards for valor.

Captain Picard chose Data for his unique abilities, which Picard thought would enhance any bridge crew or Away Team. Picard believes that Data offers him a voice of reason, and that is the kind of advice Picard values. Since his arrival on the *Enterprise*, Data has assumed the role of third in command.

Personality:

Data is the equivalent of a walking ship library. He has knowledge of everything known to the Federation. As such, he is an invaluable member of the *Enterprise*.

Data is very literal and can be confused by human idioms and figures of speech. His own attempts to use those idioms are never very successful.

Data also attempts to emulate human emotions, but most of his attempts are not very successful. When he returned to Omicron Theta and discovered his "brother," Lore, he learned that his design specifically prevented him from ever fully blending with human beings. This has not stopped him from trying, however.

Data has a strong liking for children, mostly because he identifies with their curiosity and fascination with life. Data is fiercely loyal to Starfleet, its goals, and his fellow officers.

Name: TROI, Deanna
Rank/Title: Lieutenant Commander, *USS Enterprise*
Position: Ship's Counselor

Race: Betazoid/Human
Age: 29
Sex: Female

Attributes:

STR	47	CHAR	70
INT	63	LUC	55
END	56	PSI	60
DEX	64		

Combat Statistics:
   To-Hit Numbers–   Bare Hand Damage: 1D10
      Modern: 37   AP: 10
      HTH: 42

Significant Skills	Rating
Administration	56
Artistic Expression	
Clothing Design	20
Communication Systems Operation	45
Computer Operation	69
Computer Technology	22
Damage Control Procedures	23
Instruction	65
Language	
Klingonaase	21
Vulcan	30
Leadership	21
Life Sciences	
Xenobiology	22
Life Support Systems Technology	19
Medical Sciences	
General Medicine, Human	15
Marksmanship, Modern	37
Negotiations/Diplomacy	80
Personal Combat	
Armed	17
Unarmed	20
Shuttlecraft Pilot	25
Social Sciences	
Federation Culture/History	56
Federation Law	50
Political Science	76
Starship Sensors	32
Transporter Operation Procedures	19

Distinguishing Physical Traits:

Deanna Troi is of medium build and height, and is half-Human and half-Betaziod. She usually wears her hair in a traditional Betazoid bun, but occasionally lets it down. Her voice is deep and heavily accented.

Brief Personal History:

Deanna was born on Betazed, the home world of the Betazoids. Her mother was a native of Betazed and her father was a Starfleet officer assigned to the planet. Her only living relative is her mother, whom she visits when leave is possible.

During a previous assignment, she became intimate friends with William Riker. The relationship ended when he was reassigned. Riker's reappearance in her life aboard the *Enterprise* was a shock for her, and she is slowly adjusting to it.

When the post of Ship's Counselor became available aboard the new *USS Enterprise*, she requested transfer immediately, hoping that this new class and its mission would provide her with more contacts with other cultures. She was very impressed by Captain Picard, particularly with his level of emotional control and inner calm.

Personality:

Troi fits in well with the multi-racial environment of the *Enterprise*, and enjoys the challenges of service aboard the ship.

As an expert in human engineering, Troi is privy to the secrets and fears of all the crew, but she never abuses this knowledge. She is very circumspect when offering advice to anyone and will never undermine the authority of the Captain or anyone else in the chain of command with an ill-phrased suggestion.

Name: YAR, Tasha (deceased)
Rank/Title: Lieutenant, *USS Enterprise*
Position: Security Chief

Race: Human
Age: 26
Sex: Female

Attributes:

STR	70	CHAR	50
INT	59	LUC	07
END	67	PSI	09
DEX	84		

Combat Statistics:

To-Hit Numbers–   Bare Hand Damage: 1D10+3
　　Modern: 75   AP: 10
　　HTH: 82

Significant Skills	Rating
Administration	44
Communication Systems Operation	38
Computer Operation	70
Damage Control Procedures	72
Deflector Shield Operation	67
Environmental Suit Operations	13
Instruction	60
Language	
Klingonaase	15
Leadership	30
Life Sciences	
Genetics	09
Marksmanship, Modern	70
Medical Sciences	
General Medicine, Human	20
Negotiation/Diplomacy	20
Personal Combat	
Armed	80
Unarmed	81
Personal Weapons Technology	50
Planetary Survival	20
Security Procedures	85
Shuttlecraft Pilot	23
Small Unit Tactics	68
Social Sciences	
Federation Culture/History	30
Federation Law	40
Sports	
Parrises Squares	39
Starship Combat Strategy/Tactics	54
Starship Sensors	44
Starship Weaponry Operation	67
Transporter Operation Procedures	68
Warp Drive Technology	16

Distinguishing Physical Characteristics:

Tasha Yar is short and fit. She wears her blond hair short, and she is one of the more attractive members of the *Enteprise*'s crew.

Brief Personal History:

Tasha Yar led a tragic early life. She was born on Hokma V, a remote mining world in the midst of political turmoil. When she was young, miners staged a bloody coup that killed the Federation ambassador and the head of the planetary government. Tasha's parents died in the anarchy that followed. Bands of armed men raped and ravaged the population of Hokma V, and burnings and lootings were a nightly occurrence.

She spent most of her early life hiding from the rape gangs and learning to survive in the worst possible conditions. She became a stern and determined individual.

As Security Chief, Yar performed well in several crises aboard the *Enterprise*, and she received a number of commendations. Her life was cut short on Yagra II, however, when she was killed during an operation to rescue Deanna Troi.

Pesonality:

Tasha Yar reacts with great emotion, or even violence, in tense situations. In other circumstances, she is very logical and professional.

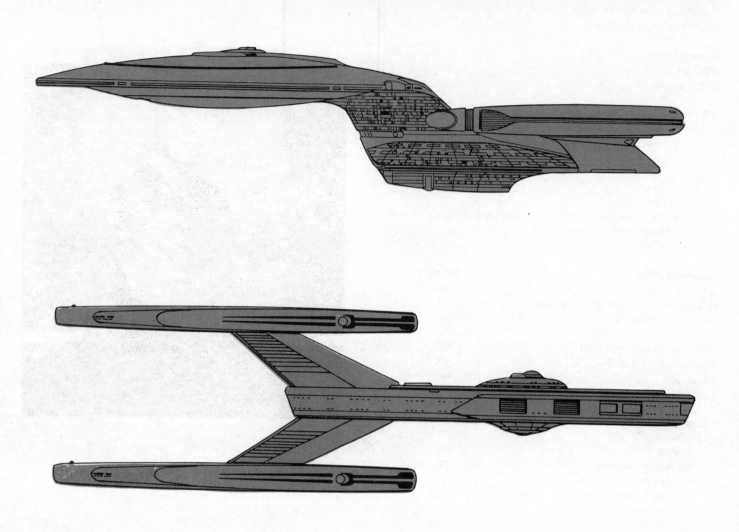

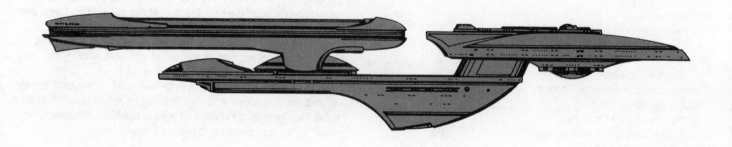

NOT TO SCALE

The first season of *The Next Generation* has introduced a variety of new ships. Technological improvements have made these ships bigger, more powerful, and faster than their predecessors. These differences are due primarily to a major improvement in warp drive technology.

Like many technological advances, the improved warp engines fostered numerous changes in technical jargon. The most pervasive one has been the redefining of warp factor. Under the old system, a given warp factor was equal to the factor cubed times the speed of light. Warp Factor 3, for example, was equal to 3 x 3 x 3, or 27 times the speed of light(c). Because the new engines could propel a ship at unheard-of-speeds, the old warp factors became unwieldy. For example, a cruiser could achieve a speed of 32,768c. Under the old system, the ship would be traveling at warp factor 32, a cumbersome number.

Recognizing the problem, Starfleet changed the standard so that a given warp factor was equal to the factor raised to the fifth power, making the refitted maximum speed Warp 8 (8 x 8 x 8 x 8 x 8).

Following are game stats and a brief description of starships shown during the first season of *STAR TREK:* **The Next Generation**. Please note that all of the ships have being equipped with improved warp drives and that all speeds use the new warp scale rather than the older scale.

WARP DRIVE ADVANCEMENTS

With the operational failure of the transwarp drive propulsion system, Federation engineers went back to improving the basic warp technology. Conventional wisdom held that warp drive technology had reached its upper limits and that no major breakthroughs would occur. As has been the case since time immemorial, conventional wisdom was wrong.

A research team headed by Dr. Katherine Ballantine created a computer model that postulated using two "mated" pairs of warp engines, with a total of four separate warp field generators, each casting a single warp field ahead of an ongoing craft in a perfectly timed sequence of events. This resulted in a vessel moving continually from one warp field into another, with the constant "shifting" (which can be observed as a sudden doppler shift in visible light) acting as a multiplier effect.

The results were astonishing. Warp-drive technology had never been able to propel an object faster than 2,744 times the speed of light. Using this model, Dr. Ballantine discovered that speeds approaching 100,000 times the speed of light were possible. Also, this model helped her to prove that 100,000 times the speed of light was an upper limit in this universe.

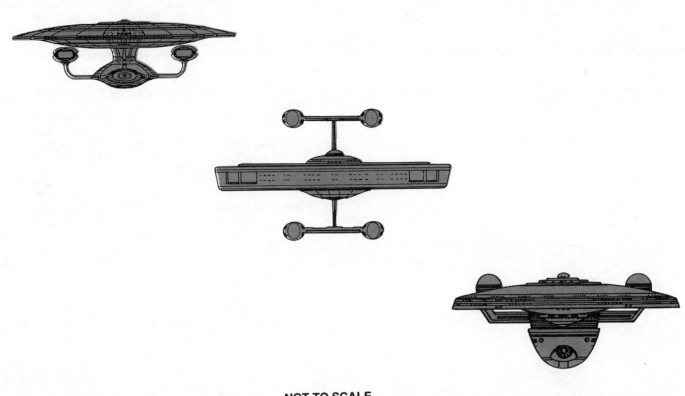

NOT TO SCALE

GALAXY CLASS STARSHIP
USS ENTERPRISE (NCC–1701–D)

Construction Data:
Model Number—	I
Date Entering Service—	40301.2

Hull Data:
Superstructure Points—	98
Damage Chart—	C
Size	
Length—	642.5 m
Width—	467 m
Height—	137.5 m
Weight—	3,000,000 mt
Cargo	
Cargo Units—	500 SCU
Cargo Capacity—	25,000 mt
Landing Capability—	No

Equipment Data:
Control Computer Type—	M-9A Duotronics AICS
Transporters—	
standard 6-person	20
cargo, large	3
cargo, small	5

Other Data:
Crew—	900+
Passengers—	800 maximum (300 standard)
Shuttlecraft—	12

Engines and Power Data:
Total Power Units Available—	120(160 w/saucer)

Star Drive Section—
Total Power Units Available—	120
Movement Point Ratio—	7/1
Warp Engine Type—	FIWE-1
Number—	2
Power Units Available—	40
Stress Charts—	E/F
Maximum Safe Cruising Speed—	Warp 6
Emergency Speed—	Warp 9.95
Impulse Engine Type—	FIG-3
Power Units Available—	40

Saucer Section (Emergency Disconnection Only)—
Total Power Units Available—	40
Movement Point Ratio—	4/1
Impulse Engine Type—	FIG-3
Power Units Available—	40

Weapons and Firing Data:
Beam Weapon Type—	FH-15
Number—	1
Firing Arcs—	300-degree Collimator Arc f/p/s
Firing Chart—	Y
Maximum Power—	30
Damage Modifiers—	
+3	(1–11)
+2	(12–20)
+1	(21–24)
Missile Weapon Type —	FP–10
Number—	4
Firing Arcs–	3 f/p/s, 1a
Firing Chart–	S
Power to Arm–	1
Damage – .	30

Main Saucer Section (Emergency Disconnection Only)
Beam Weapon Type —	FH-11
Number—	1
Firing Arcs—	300-degree Collimator (Arc f/p/s)
Maximum Power—	10
Damage Modifiers—	
+3	(1–10)
+2	(11–17)
+1	(18–24)

Shields Data:
Deflector Shield Type—	FSS-M
Shield Point Ratio—	1/4
Maximum Shield Power—	22

Combat Efficiency:
D—	300+ (est.)
WDF—	250+ (est.)

Operational Capabilities
Cruising Range	25,570
Expected Lifetime	35 standard years
Average Time until Resupply	12 standard years
Estimated Time between Refittings	15 standard years
Power Generation:	
Primary	Third-Generation Multi-Field Warp Drive
Secondary	Chiokis Fusion Reactors, A-D
Tertiary	Mark-9 Solar Battery Collectors

Power Output:
Maximum Speed	Warp 9.95
Interval From Subspace to Warp 1	1.2 microseconds

Computer System:
Type and Manufacturer	Duotronics M-9A AICS Command System
Storage Capacity	125,575,500 terra bytes
Average Response Time	0.3478 nanoseconds

Sensor Systems Capabilities:
Primary Sensor Detector Radius	3.3 parsecs
Automated Telemetry Control Radius	2.5 parsecs

Transporter Range:
	40,000 kilometers direct line-of-sight

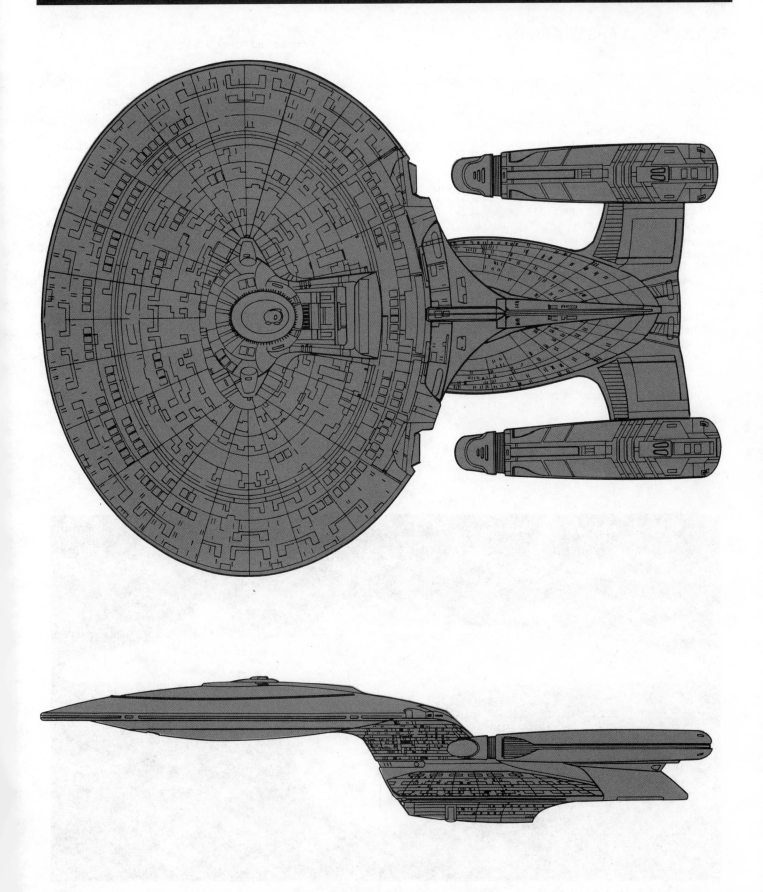

EXCELSIOR CLASS STARSHIP

Construction Data:

Model Number—	MK III
Date Entering Service—	37341.4

Hull Data:

Superstructure Points—	40
Damage Chart—	C

Size

Length—	467 m
Width—	186 m
Height—	78 m
Weight—	239,645 mt

Cargo

Cargo Units—	100 SCU
Cargo Capacity—	500 mt
Landing Capability—	None

Equipment Data:

Control Computer Type—	M-8

Transporters—

standard 6-person	6
emergency 22-person	6
cargo	3

Other Data:

Crew	802
Additional Accommodations	40
Shuttlecraft	20

Engines And Power Data:

Total Power Units Available—	128
Movement Point Ratio—	6/1
Warp Engine Type—	FIWAI
Number—	2
Power Units Available—	48
Stress Charts—	D/F
Maximum Safe Cruising Speed—	Warp 6
Emergency Speed—	Warp 8
Impulse Engine Type—	FIG-2
Power Units Available—	32

Weapons and Firing Data:

Beam Weapon Type—	FH-11
Number—	8 in 5 banks
Firing Arcs—	1 f/p, 2 f, 1 f/s, 2 p/a, 2 s/a
Firing Chart—	Y
Maximum Power—	10

Damage Modifiers—

+3	(1 – 10)
+2	(11 – 17)
+1	(18 – 24)

Missile Weapon Type—	FP-4
Number—	6
Firing Arcs—	1 f, 2 f/p, 2 f/s, 1 a
Firing Chart—	S
Power To Arm—	1
Damage—	20

Shields Data:

Deflector Shield Type—	FSS
Shield Point Ratio—	1/4
Maximum Shield Power—	20

Combat Efficiency:

D—	179.2
WDF—	160.6

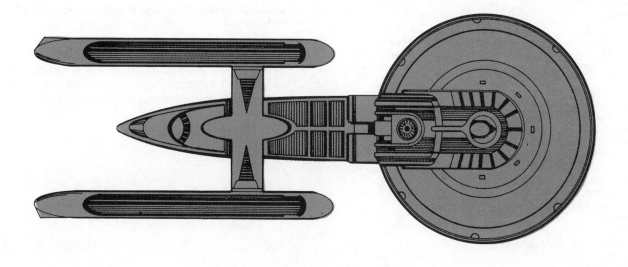

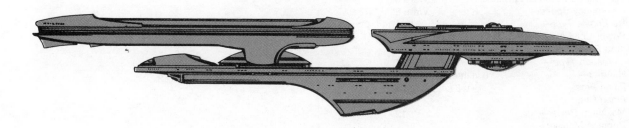

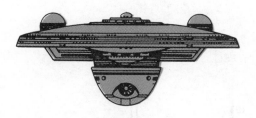

CONSTELLATION CLASS STARSHIP

Construction Data:

Model Number—	I
Date Entering Service—	38002.5

Hull Data:

Superstructure Points—	33
Damage Chart—	C

Size

Length—	310 m
Width—	140 m
Height—	94 m
Weight—	208,993 mt

Cargo

Cargo Units—	125 SCU
Cargo Capacity—	6,250 mt
Landing Capability—	None

Equipment Data:

Control Computer Type—	M-6A

Transporters—

standard 6-person	4
emergency 12-person	4
cargo, large	1
cargo, small	2

Other Data:

Crew—	350
Additional Accommodations—	20
Shuttlecraft—	8

Engines and Power Data:

Total Power Units Available—	92
Movement Point Ratio—	4/1
Warp Engine Type—	FIWD-2
Number—	2 (4)
Power Units Available—	40
Stress Charts—	E/F
Maximum Safe Cruising Speed—	Warp 6
Emergency Speed—	Warp 8
Impulse Engine Type—	FIF-1
Power Units Available—	12

Weapons and Firing Data:

Beam Weapon Type—	FH-14
Number—	6 in three banks of 2
Firing Arcs—	2 s/f, 2 p/f, 2 a
Firing Chart—	T
Maximum Power—	12

Damage Modifiers—

+3	(1–5)
+2	(6–12)
+1	(13–18)

Missile Weapon Type—	FP-4
Number—	4
Firing Arcs—	2 f/p/s, 2 a/p/s
Firing Chart—	S
Power to Arm—	1
Damage—	20

Shields Data:

Deflector Shield Type—	FSQ
Shield Point Ratio—	1/4
Maximum Shield Power—	18

Combat Efficiency:

D—	193.76
WDF—	104.60

Notes:

With the venerable *Constitution* Class design stretched to its limits, any further advances would require a totally new hull design. Recognizing this limitation, Starfleet designers came up with the *Constellation* Class starship. The *Constellation* was a radical design departure because of its unique four-engine nacelle configuration. The class has distinguished itself, particularly in the action involving the *USS Stargazer* under the command of Captain J.L. Picard. It was in this action that the Captain introduced the now famous Picard Maneuver. Of the 26 *Constellation* Class cruisers constructed, 20 are still in service, 3 have been destroyed, 1 scrapped, and 2 lost (though one of these was subsequently recovered and decommissioned).

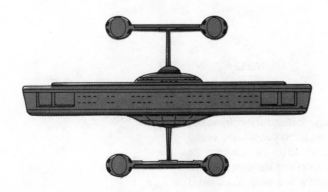

SCOUT CLASS SCIENCE RESEARCH VESSEL STARSHIP

Construction Data:

Model Number—	I
Date Entering Service—	38502

Hull Data:

Superstructure Points—	9
Damage Chart—	C
Size	
Length—	180 m
Width—	105 m
Height—	62 m
Weight—	151,173 mt
Cargo	
Cargo Units—	200 SCU
Cargo Capacity—	10,000 mt

Equipment Data:

Control Computer Type—	M-1
Transporters—	
standard 6-person	2
emergency 12-person	5
cargo, large	2
cargo, small	2

Other Data:

Crew—	80
Mission Specialists—	10
Shuttlecraft—	4

Engines and Power Data:

Total Power Units Available—	52
Movement Point Ratio—	4/1
Warp Engine Type—	FIWC-1
Number—	2
Power Units Available—	20
Stress Charts—	D/E
Maximum Safe Cruising Speed—	Warp 6
Emergency Speed—	Warp 8
Impulse Engine Type—	FIF-1
Power Units Available—	12

Weapons and Firing Data:

Beam Weapon Type—	FH-8
Number—	3
Firing Arcs—	2 f/p/s, 1 a
Firing Chart—	T
Maximum Power—	5
Damage Modifiers—	
+2	(1–10)
+1	(11–18)

Shields Data:

Deflector Shield Type—	FSF
Shield Point Ratio—	1/2
Maximum Shield Power—	8

Combat Efficiency:

D—	102.88
WDF—	12.90

Notes:

An upscaled version of the old *Gagarin* Class science vessel, the *Scout* deep-space science and research vessel has vastly improved facilities and instrumentation, to better perform its missions. The *Scout* is designed to provide an extensive geological, biological, and cartographic survey of newly discovered worlds and to serve as a manned deep-space probe of astronomical and astrophysical phenomena on station for long periods of time. Though no longer in production, most of these vessels remain in service.

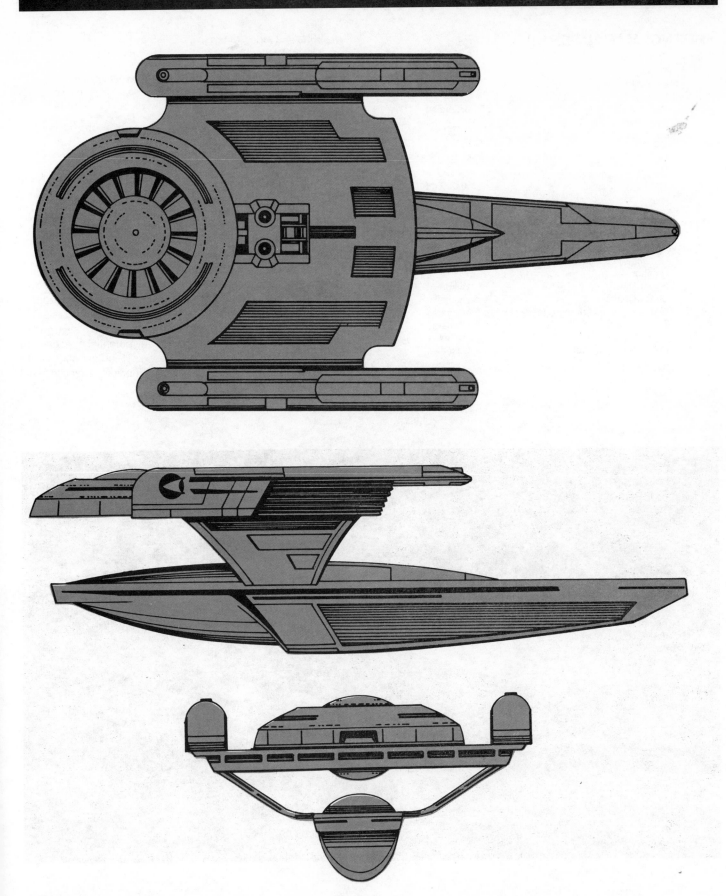

FERENGI *MARAUDER*

Construction Data:

Number Constructed—	Unknown
Intelligence Estimate Rating—	B

Hull Data:

Superstructure Points—	250 estimated
Damage Chart—	C

Size

Length—	580 m
Width—	500 m
Height—	135 m
Weight—	200,000 mt

Other Data:

Crew—	500 estimated

Engines and Power Data:

Total Power Units Available—	150–180 estimated
Movement Point Ratio—	4/1
Warp Engine Type—	FRNW-1
Number—	2
Power Units Available—	Unknown
Stress Charts—	Unknown
Maximum Safe Cruising Speed—	Warp 6 estimated
Emergency Speed—	Warp 8 estimated
Impulse Engine Type—	FRNI-1
Power Units Available—	Unknown

Weapons and Firing Data:

Beam Weapon Type—	Plasma Disrupters
Number—	5
Firing Arcs—	Assume a full 360-degree arc
Firing Chart—	T estimated
Power Range—	10–14

Shields Data:

Deflector Shield Type—	FRNS-1
Shield Point Ratio—	1/3
Maximum Shield Power—	20 estimated

Combat Efficiency: Unable to calculate at this time

Notes:

This mammoth vessel may be a combination combat vessel and trader/acquisition/storage ship. The *Marauder* Class Ferengi cruiser appears to have considerable power reserve, though the exact nature of the vessel's power-generation system is not known. Evidence obtained from declassified reports points to a strong shielding capability, but one that can only be projected over a limited arc at any given time. This vessel does, however, appear to use an advanced form of combination tractor beam-stasis field projection system that can hold an enemy craft in relative immobility if one should stray too close. In any potential engagement between Federation and Ferengi vessels, Starfleet officers are warned to engage the Ferengi at long to medium ranges to avoid this weapon's potential.

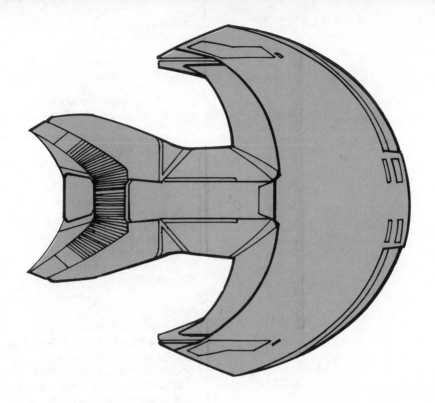

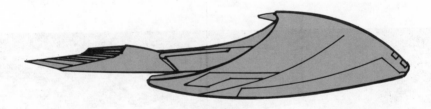

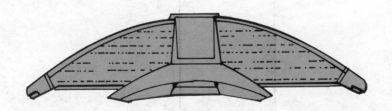

ROMULAN "WARBIRD" CLASS STARSHIP

Construction Data:

Intelligence Estimate Rating—	B

Hull Data:

Superstructure Points—	145
Damage Chart—	B
Size	
Length—	455 m
Width—	194 m
Height—	102 m
Weight—	225,000 mt
Cargo	
Cargo Units—	185 SCU est
Cargo Capacity—	9,250 MT
Landing Capacity—	None

Equipment Data:

Control Computer Type—	Unknown
Transporters—	Unknown
Cloaking Device Type—	RCF
Power Requirement—	75

Other Data:

Crew—	400 est
Troops—	300 est
Shuttlecraft—	4–6 est

Engines and Power Data:

Total Power Units Available—	130
Movement Point Ratio—	3/1
Warp Engine Type—	RIWD-1B
Number—	2
Power Units Available—	50
Stress Charts—	D/E
Maximum Safe Cruising Speed–	Warp 6
Emergency Speed—	Warp 9
Impulse Engine Type—	RIG-V
Power Units Available—	30

Weapons and Firing Data:

Beam Weapon Type—	RWW-H
Number—	10
Firing Arcs—	4 f, 4 p/s, 2a assumed
Firing Chart	T
Power Range	10
Damage Modifiers—	
+3	(1–15)
+2	(16–22)
+1	(23–30)
Missile Weapon Type—	RTA-E
Number	6
Firing Arc—	4 f/p/s, 2 a
Firing Chart—	N
Power to Arm—	1
Damage—	20

Shields Data:

Deflector Shield Type—	RSM-5
Shield Point Ratio—	1/1
Maximum Shield Power—	18

Combat Efficiency: Not yet rated

Notes:

The Romulan *Warbird* Class starship appears to be the latest in a long line of Romulan advances, culminating in a superior fighting vessel able to match the best the Federation has to offer. Like the rest of the Romulan fleet, little is known of this class of ship. Most data is from sensor scans by the *USS Enterprise,* which recently encountered one in Federation space. From these scans, a profile of this class and its capabilities has been constructed. While most of the technological data is incomplete, it is known that Romulan cloaking technology has kept pace with advancements in Federation sensor technology.

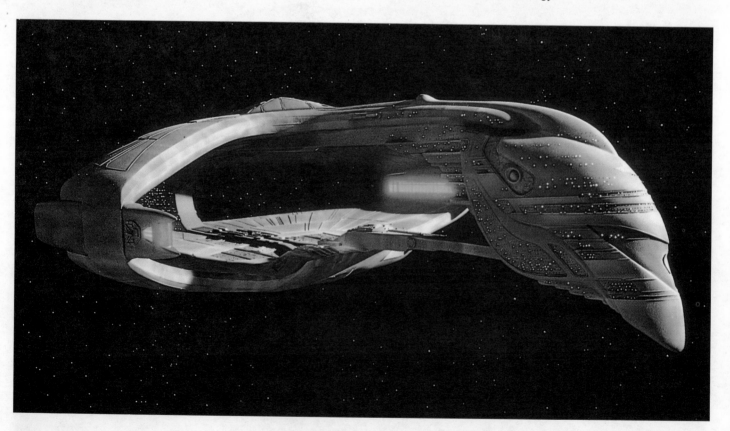

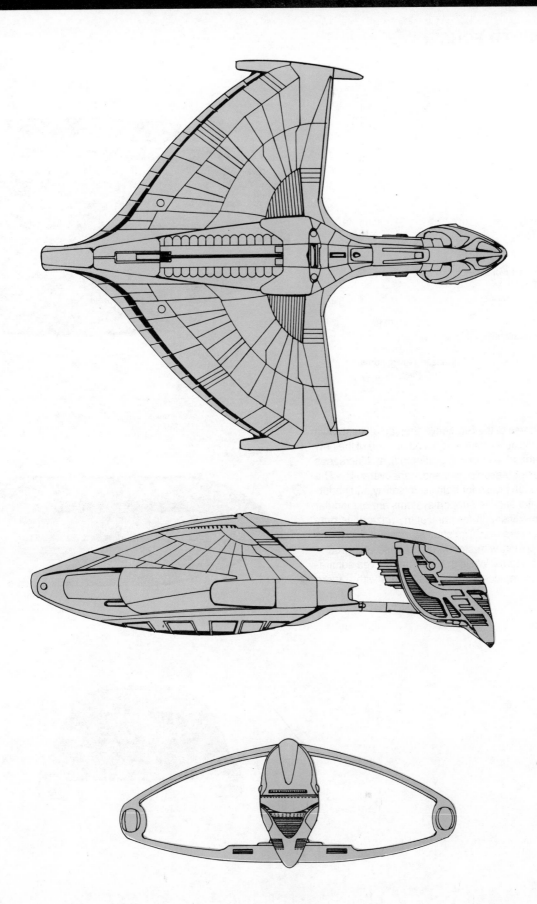

STANDARD SHUTTLECRAFT

Construction Data:

    Model Number—   II

    Date Entering Service—   38507

Hull Data:

    Superstructure Points—   1

    Damage Chart—   C

    Size

        Length—   30 m

        Width—   8 m

        Height—   12 m

        Weight—   820 mt

    Cargo

        Cargo Units   2 SCU

        Cargo Capacity   100 mt

    Landing Capability—   Yes

Other Data:

    Crew—   2

    Additional Accommodations—   6

Engines and Power Data:

    Total Power Units Available—   3

    Movement Point Ratio—   1/4

    Impulse Engine Type—   FMIB-3

        Power Units Available–   3

Shields Data:

    Deflector Shield Type—   Enhanced Navigational Deflectors Only

    Shield Strength—   2

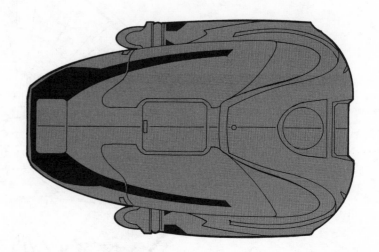

Notes:

This is the workhorse of the Starfleet's shuttlecraft fleet. Built to replace older models, this craft takes full advantage of the new generation of micro-impulse engines, trading minimal increases in space allocation for increased power and maneuverability. The shuttlecraft has won high praise for both its versatility and endurance. Its environmental and life-support systems are of modular design, simplifying modification for particularly hazardous duty when no parent craft is present. The shuttle's computer systems are also capable of linking with standard star base and ground navigational control systems. While the S-20 has served admirably, it will probably be replaced in the near future with a more advanced design.

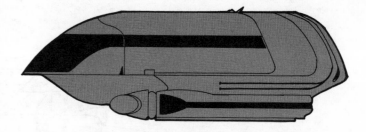

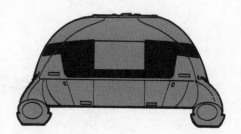

The first season of *STAR TREK: The Next Generation* introduces many new pieces of equipment. Some of these will make significant changes in the play of *STAR TREK: The Role Playing Game.*

HOLODECK

A particularly attractive feature of the *Galaxy* Class starship is the numerous holodeck units. Drawing on revolutionary advances in matter transformation, the holodeck uses holodiodes and the ship's transporter control systems to rearrange bulk matter into a predetermined pattern. In this manner, specially constructed Holodeck environments can be altered to resemble any of several thousand locations drawn from Federation computer memory banks. Moreover, holodeck units can use the ship's central computer to generate patterns of organic lifeforms, including the appearance and mannerisms of living beings. The user can simulate encounters with life-like images of persons both living and deceased with surprising accuracy. Such capabilities also provide for instruction while the user trains in simulated conditions involving interaction with computer-generated personnel, friend or foe. The individual can re-create nearly perfect simulated environments, conversing with loved ones or famous individuals from any time period. Moreover, with prior programming, an individual can construct an "alternate-reality" world of the imagination.

The holodeck is an excellent gamemaster plot device. In essence, the holodeck is the 24th century's equivalent of a roleplaying game. The holodeck can be integrated with a ship-based adventure, such as "The Big Goodbye" or "11001001," or be the site for an "alternate world" adventure that the characters are playing. It might be a bit difficult for the players to role play *STAR TREK* characters who are roleplaying 18th century pirates, but the existence of the holodeck can be used to expand your players' roleplaying experience.

STARFLEET PERSONAL EQUIPMENT

The following pieces of equipment are common throughout Starfleet. All personnel can recognize this equipment, and unless otherwise noted, understand its basic operation.

COMMUNICATORS

The old hand-held communicator has been replaced by a small, lightweight device worn on the chest. The gold alloy of this piece of equipment acts as a conductor, while the base of the insignia sends a constant readout of the wearer's life signs to the ship's computer. If life-sign readings indicate a problem, the computer will alert the Chief Medical officer and the Bridge Duty Officer. All crewmembers wear the device as part of their uniform.

The communicator's maximum range is 40,000 kilometers.

SCIENCE TRICORDER

The tricorder is a standard-issue, multi-functional device that provides environmental information to Away Team members. The tricorder acts as a sensor, and collects data for later review. As a standard Away Team-device, the tricorder is used for close-range sensor sweeps of an area. With a simple push of a button, the Tricorder can be configured to gather information on the geological, meteorological, or biological features of a region.

Using this device, players can detect energy sources and types, analyze the physical and chemical composition of an item, locate and identify lifeforms, and collect data for further evaluation back aboard the ship.

The tricorder·can tie into any Federation starship for a data link with the ship's main library computer. It carries an extensive library of its own and can be programmed with specific data bases before any mission.

Characters using the tricorder in an attempt to analyze data receive a +10 modifier.

SCIENCE TRICORDER
Length:
Extended: 16 cm
Folded: 12 cm
Width: 9.2 cm
Height: 4 cm
Weight: .86 kg
Scanning Range:
Terrain: 8 km
Life Form: 6 km
Subterranean: 500 m
Meteorological: 25 km
Analysis Time: 15 AP (can be accumulated over turns)
Transmitting Range: 45,000 km
Power: 1 Energy Cell (96 hours constant use)
AP to Change Energy Cell: 2
Minimum Skills: 05 in skill area

MEDICAL TRICORDER

Similar in layout and design to the science tricorder, the medical tricorder can scan lifeforms within five kilometers, analyzing brain-wave activity as well as such normal vital functions as respiration and blood pressure. It comes with a diagnostic wand as a standard feature.

The medical tricorder has the same emergency features for broadcasting and lock-on for transporting as the science tricorder. It has compartments for tissue and blood analysis, and its library carries emergency treatment information on more than a hundred known sapient and other lifeforms for comparison analysis.

A player using a medical tricorder receives a +10 for any diagnostic attempts that he makes, and a +5 for any form of medical research.

MEDICAL TRICORDER
Length:
Extended: 16 cm
Folded: 12 cm
Width: 9.2 cm
Height: 4 cm
Weight: .92 kg
Scanning Range:
Lifeform: 5 km
Chemical: 200 m
Radiation: 3 km
Vital Signs: 20 m
Analysis Time:
Blood: 10 AP (can be accumulated over turns)
Lifeform: 14 AP (can be accumulated over turns)
Vital Signs: 8 AP (can be accumulated over turns)
Transmitting Range: 40,000 km
Power: 1 Energy Cell (80 hours constant use)
AP to Change Energy Cell: 2

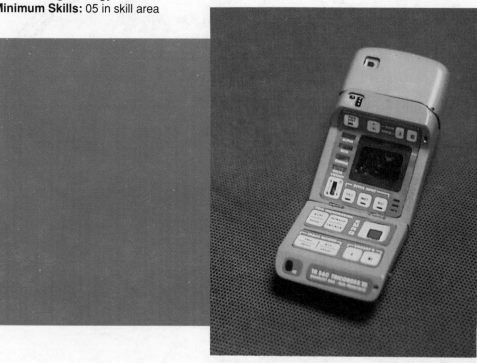

SECURITY TRICORDER

This tricorder catalogues the energy and power of weapons used by hundreds of civilizations. It also can identify and decipher many forms of codes.

The security tricorder monitors lifeform movements and analyzes their intent, based on the tactics stored in its library. It also detects energy buildups for weapons tracking, and then relays this information to the starship for targeting.

A security tricorder gives a character a +10 when attempting to analyze any weapon system, determine the technological level of the creature using it, the type of damage to be expected, and effective countermeasures.

SECURITY TRICORDER

Length:
  Extended: 16 cm
  Folded: 12 cm
Width: 9.2 cm
Height: 4 cm
Weight: .94 kg
Scanning Range:
  Lifeform: 8 km
  Energy: 10 km
  Subterranean: 200 m
Analysis Time:
  Lifeform: 8 AP (can be accumulated over turns)
  Tactics: 5 AP (can be accumulated over turns)
  Weapons: 7 AP (can be accumulated over turns)
Transmitting Range: 40,000 km
Power: 1 Energy Cell (95 hours constant use)
AP to Change Energy Cell: 2
Minimum Skills:
  Security Procedures: 05

PHASERS

TYPE I HAND PHASER

This small, hand-held, easily concealed sidearm combines the latest in microcircuitry and energy-flow alignment techniques. Indeed, the Type I Hand Phaser boasts a maximum power output three times that of earlier models. Characterized by its wafer-thin styling, the Type I phaser is less than 10 centimeters long and 2.5 centimeters wide. Inside this slim housing are two power converter chips that can be recharged from a portable energy pack or from an adaptable connector on standard tricorders. The surface plate of the Type I Phaser contains two pressure-sensitive energy regulators; the left-hand activator controls beam width and the right-hand plate controls beam intensity. In normal use, the user can select up to eight power settings, from light stun to total vaporization.

This phaser is standard-issue for Bridge and Engineering personnel and for diplomatic Away Team missions.

Length: 9.8 cm
Width: 2.5 cm
Height: 2.0 cm
Weight: .9 kg
Power: 2 Energy Clips
Maximum Range: 120 squares (180 meters)

TYPE II HAND PHASER

When ship's personnel are expecting danger, the heavier Type II Hand Phaser is issued. With its broom-handle design and width-mounted power core, this bulky but light weapon is usually worn in a velcro hip-holster that doubles as a recharging unit. The Type II Hand Phaser functions as a two-in-one system. It combines two interlocking phased-particle beams in a collimator field to produce a single-charged particle beam. The resulting firepower is far greater than in earlier models, and is capable of vaporizing 100 cubic meters of rock. By altering the frequency of the beam's dispersal pattern, the Type II's power collimator can also reduce the electron flow, generating a simple laser or a variety of plasma-like beams suitable for use in non-combat emergencies when communications or energy transmissions are required. The Type II phaser has eight more power settings than the Type I phaser. Static tests have shown that the weapon can fire at full power for two and a half hours before power is completely drained.

TYPE II HAND PHASER

Length: 28 centimeters
Width: 8 centimeters
Height: 4 centimeters
Weight: 1.5 kilogram
Power: 6 Energy Clips in handle
Maximum Range: 130 squares (195 meters)

In addition to stun and heavy stun, non-lethal settings of Starfleet phasers now also include energy-wave disruption ("Arsenal of Freedom"). See the **Echo Poppa 607** description for a full explanation.

It takes 1AP to change the Energy Clip on a phaser. Energy Clips can be recharged at any power station on a starship or from any tricorder. Recharging an Energy Clip drains the power from a tricorder.

The same skills and die rolls are used for combat as in the original roleplaying game.

ENGINEERING KIT

This is an Engineering Specialist's tool box. It is a portable energy-analysis station and repair kit for mechanical, electrical, or structural difficulties. It provides sufficient tools and diagnostic equipment to repair most items aboard ship.

A character with an engineering kit receives a +5 modifier when attempting to repair a piece of equipment.

ENGINEERING KIT

Length: 25 cm
Width: 8 cm
Height: 18 cm
Weight: 2.6 kg
Minimum Skill:
Mechanical Engineering: 20

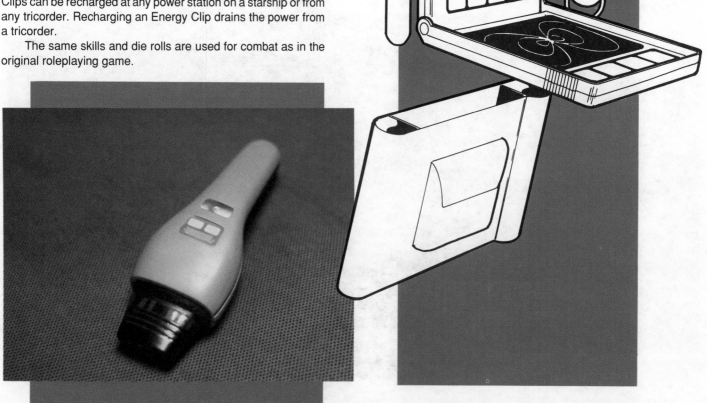

MEDICAL EQUIPMENT

DIAGNOSTIC BED

Modern starships have the new-model diagnostic bed, which displays all information about a patient on the body cover and on the adjoining wall panel. The bed itself contains a sensor-net weaving that gathers information from all parts of the body. Alarms indicate abnormal readings, positive identification of illnesses, and potential long-terms threats to the patient.

A fold-away platform can be positioned over the patient and holds a standard sterilization field, dispensing systems for intravenous medicines, a cardiovascular stimulator, and an auto-respiratory stimulator.

A player with the minimum skill level receives a +20 modifier for any diagnosis that he is attempting, along with the normal healing advantages for having a fully equipped medical facility available.

Minimum Skill:
General Medicine: 20

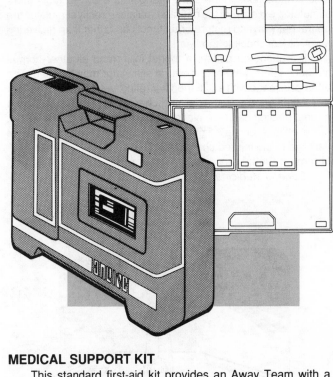

MEDICAL SUPPORT KIT

This standard first-aid kit provides an Away Team with a diagnostic wand; a hypo spray; three 100cc ampules each of a respiratory stimulant, pain suppressant, and general stimulant; four 4.5-centimeter plasticene splints; sterilized pressure bandages; fluorocarbon skin-graft replacements; anti-radiation tablets, water purification tablets; and spare data crystals and power packs for a medical tricorder.

The kit gives a character a +5 modifier when applying emergency first aid.

Minimum Skill:
General Medicine: 10

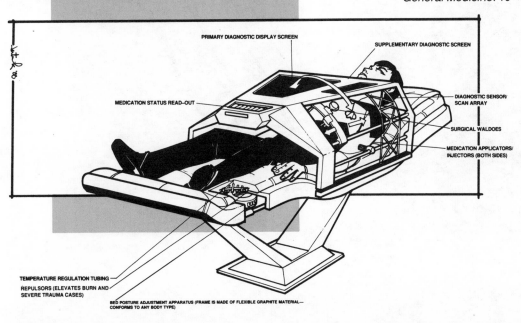

PRIMARY DIAGNOSTIC DISPLAY SCREEN

SUPPLEMENTARY DIAGNOSTIC SCREEN

MEDICATION STATUS READ-OUT

DIAGNOSTIC SENSOR/ SCAN ARRAY

SURGICAL WALDOES

MEDICATION APPLICATORS/ INJECTORS (BOTH SIDES)

TEMPERATURE REGULATION TUBING

REPULSORS (ELEVATES BURN AND SEVERE TRAUMA CASES)

BED POSTURE ADJUSTMENT APPARATUS (FRAME IS MADE OF FLEXIBLE GRAPHITE MATERIAL— CONFORMS TO ANY BODY TYPE)

NEURAL STIMULATOR

The neural stimulator is used as a medical device of last resort. It functions in the same manner as a 20th-century heart stimulator, except that the neural stimulator directly stimulates the neural pathways to restore brain functions rather than delivering an electrical shock to the heart.

If a character suffers a mortal injury and all other normal methods fail to save him, a neural stimulator may be used. The attempt is made with a +25 modifier (effectively negating the Sick Bay Modifier). If successful, the character's END is now 1 and normal healing can take place. Multiple attempts can be made, but each use of the stimulator does an additional 5 points of damage to the injured character.

Minimum Skill:

General Medicine: 30

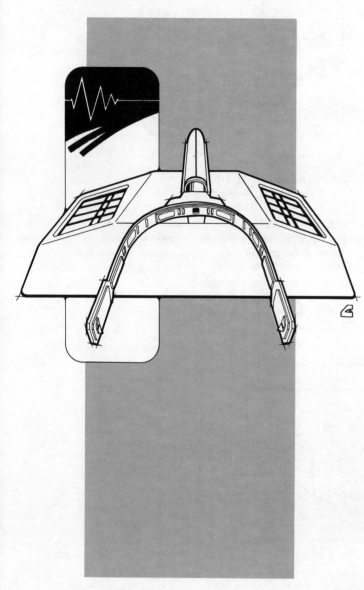

HYPO SPRAY

The standard hypo spray is capable of delivering a wide variety of drugs directly through the skin layers into the blood stream. Utilizing a compressed ultrasonic wave, the hypo spray can inject up to 200 cc's of a drug in less than 2.5 seconds. Up to 10 doses of 5 different drugs can be preloaded into the spray.

Minimum Skill:

None

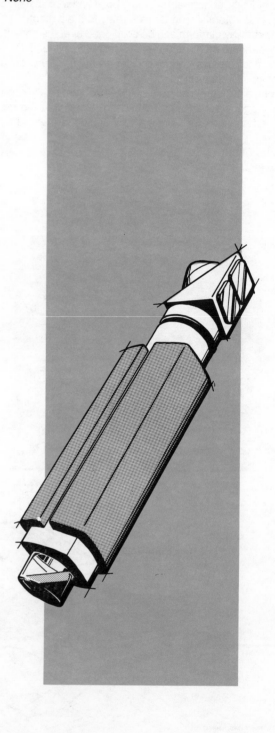

DIAGNOSTIC WAND

The Diagnostic Wand is a specialized medical sensor used by medical personnel to provide information about the medical status of a patient. With several passes of the wand, a complete medical profile of a subject can be compiled. The wand has a limited storage capacity to allow a reading to be taken and then analyzed at a latter date.

The diagnostic wand can give any medically trained character basic physiological information about a subject: blood pressure, respiration, pulse, and body temperature. Additionally, when linked with a medical computer or tricorder with a medical data base, the wand can allow a doctor to discover and localize any dysfunctions that a patient might have.

When used as a diagnostic tool, the wand gives a player an additional +5 modifier to any diagnostic rolls that he makes.

Minimum Skill:

General Medicine: 10

VISOR

A breakthrough in brain-computer linkage, the VISOR (Visual Instrument and Sensory Organ Replacement) offers the handicapped individual an alternative to sight. Microcomputer links imbedded beneath the skin at the sides of the forehead send data to a periphery image collector. Digital image processors translate analog signals from the surrounding electromagnetic spectrum, then process and send them into the vision regions of the brain via an image resonator. The result is a false color "picture" of the patient's surroundings, ranging from thermal images at the infrared end of the spectrum to the cold blues of ultraviolet. With prolonged use, however, the VISOR causes frequent headaches as the brain attempts to adjust to the "artificial" influx of information.

A VISOR-equipped character possesses the equivalent of a science tricorder's sensor ability though it is limited to line-of-sight only. The VISOR can be equipped to send a visual feed to a display unit, but its range is limited to a few kilometers ("Heart of Glory"). After each use of the VISOR as a tricorder substitute, the character should make a die roll. If the result is higher than his END, he receives 1 point of temporary damage.

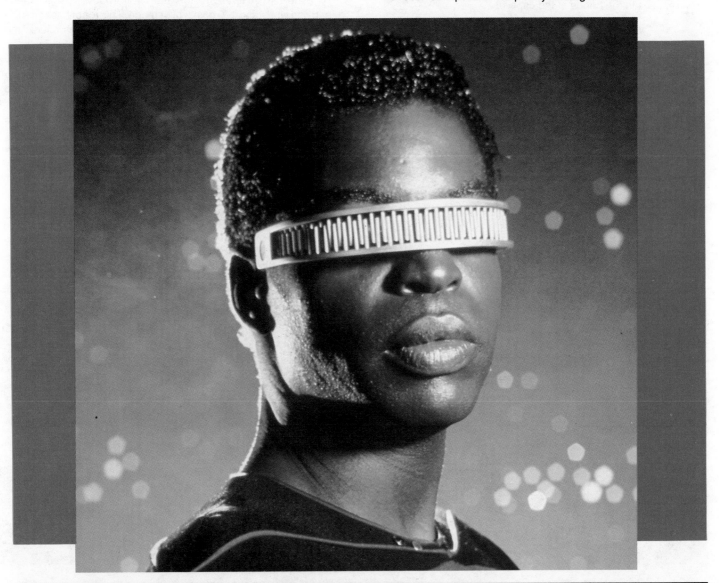

NON-STARFLEET EQUIPMENT

Following are pieces of equipment known to the Federation but not generally available to the players.

KLINGON CONCEALABLE DISRUPTOR

This rarely seen weapon consists of parts that closely resemble the parts of a Klingon warrior's uniform. In the event of capture, a Klingon can assemble the pieces into a light disruptor (treat as a Hand Disruptor -A for game purposes). Total assembly takes less than three minutes.

The parts of this device appear to be normal parts of the combat uniform, such as the belt buckle, the tips of boots, and even buttons.

If players are searching a nonplayer character equipped with this device, and specifically tell the gamemaster that they are looking for such a disruptor, they will discover it. Otherwise, the gamemaster should secretly roll against the searching character's *Security Procedures* Skill Rating with a –20 modifier. If the roll is successful, the player discovers the device. Otherwise, the device remains in the hands of the captive.

ECHO POPPA 607

Developed on the planet Minos, the Echo Poppa weapon destroyed all life there. The Echo Poppa 607 is a central computer that can generate holographic images and attack drones at a remote location.

It first reads the thoughts of its target and generates a holographic image of a trusted friend to gain information. When the target discovers the trick, the computer generates an attack drone based on the information it has (treat as Type I Hand Phaser set on Stun). The drone can also encase a target in a force field. A player with a tricorder and a phaser can break the field in 2D10 minutes. The attack drone is easily destroyed by a hit from a phaser set at a minimum of Heavy Stun.

Twelve minutes after the destruction of the drone, the computer generates a new version that builds on the new information about its target to become stronger than the first drone. The second-generation drone can dodge (treat as DEX 80), can sustain 75 points of damage, and has the firepower of a Type II Hand Phaser set on Disintegrate. If the second drone is destroyed, the computer generates a third one twelve minutes later.

The third generation of this attack robot has deflector screens and can withstand 175 points of damage. This robot has twice the firepower of a Type II Hand Phaser. Later versions double the preceding drones' deflector strength and the firepower factor.

Space-attack drones are also generated with the necessary weaponry to threaten starships, and they have full cloaking capability. Gamemasters should match the drone's firepower and shielding to the ship in orbit, but also give the drone a cloak.

Only one version of the Echo Poppa 607 is known to exist, and it has been shut down by Federation. The main computer is 8 x 4 x 5 meters, immobile, and defenseless. Statistics below are for the attack drone.

Length: 650 cm
Width: 400 cm
Height: 2 m
Weight: 340 kg (without anti-grav capabilities)
Speed: 60 KPH
Sensor Range: 20 km
Targeting Range: Varies with weapon/model of robot

FERENGI ENERGY WHIP

This is the standard sidearm carried by the Ferengi. It resembles a bull whip from Terra except that it delivers a high-energy jolt to the target's nervous system.

The whip has a limited range and is controlled by the small, baton-like handle. The whip has settings equivalent to Heavy Stun, Disrupt, and Disintegrate.

Maximum Range: 110 squares (165 meters)
Effective Range: 50 squares (75 meters)
Power: 1 Energy Cell
AP to Replace Energy Cell: 2

Any non-Ferengi attempting to use the neural energy whip must roll 1D100 against his *Personal Weapons Technology* Skill Rating. If the result is equal to or less than the skill rating, there is only a –10 modifier for use. If the result is greater than the skill rating, there is a –30 attack modifier. If the character does not have the *Personal Weapons Technology* skill, there is an automatic –40 modifier against his LUC score to use this device.

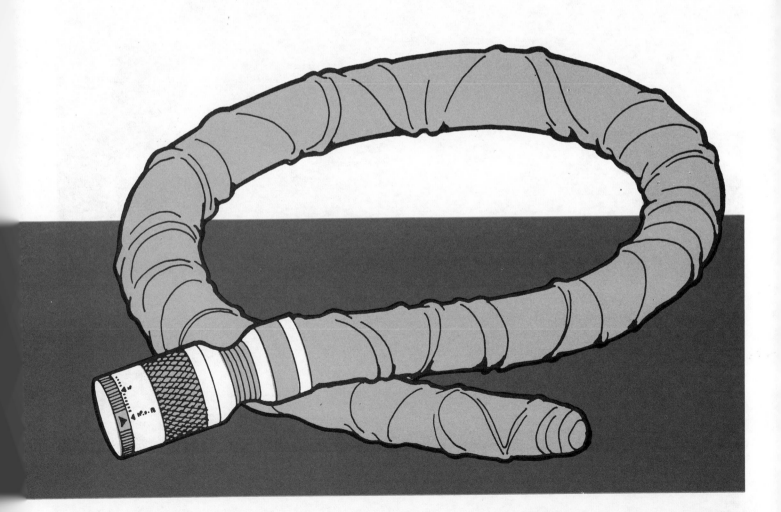

MIND CONTROL SPHERE

This system consists of two spheres, a master controller and a brain-wave amplifier. The system allows the person operating the controlling sphere to manipulate the thoughts of the victim. The sphere can create a controlled hallucination and use it to mislead the victim into all manner of actions.

The system has a very long range and is relatively simple to use. These spheres can only be set to operate on one humanoid being at a time. Destruction of either sphere ends control. The device works better if it references a strong memory of the victim. The Ferengi consider the use of such devices as illegal and do not tolerate their use at all.

The Ferengi Empire has outlawed the use of the Mind Control Sphere. These systems may be purchased on the black market, but the price is staggering.

Once the controller has activated the sphere, it takes 1D10 days for the process to begin to work on the victim. After the time lag, the intended victim must make a Saving Roll against his PSI score each day. If the controller is making use of a specific memory on the part of the victim, add 10 to the die roll. If the target fails his Saving Roll two days in a row, mind control is established.

Once the link is established, the person needs another 1D10 days operating the controlling sphere to alter the mental state of the victim. Thereafter, the controller can make the victim relive a memory, make the victim relive an altered memory, or make him experience an altered perception of reality.

The control can be broken by destroying either sphere or by making a successful Saving Roll against the character's PSI score two days in a row. The person operating the controlling sphere would then have to begin the process anew to re-establish the link.

Size:
    Controlling Sphere: 1.2 m in diameter
    Amplifying Sphere: .5 m in diameter
Weight:
    Controller: 70 kg
    Amplifier: 18 kg
Range:
    Amplifier to Victim: 10 km
    Controller to Amplifier: 100,000 km
Power: 1 Energy Clip (4 months continuous use)

This section details new races that appear in *The Next Generation*. Some of these, such as the Betazoids, present problems for the gamemaster when used as player characters. Others should be reserved for non-player characters because they are not part of the Federation.

ANGELITES

World Log: ANGEL ONE
System Data:
    System Name: Angel
    Number of Class M Worlds: 1
Planetary Data:
    Position in System: 1
    Number of Satellites: 0
    Planetary Gravity: 1.0
    Planetary Size:
        Diameter: 15,000 km
        Equatorial Circumference: 47,100 km
        Total Surface Area: 706,858,000 sq km
        Percent Land Mass: 50%
        Total Land Area: 353,429,100 sq km
    Planetary Conditions
        Length of Day: 26 hours
        Atmospheric Density: Terrestrial
        General Climate: Warm Temperate
    Mineral Content
        Normal Metals: 25%
        Radioactives: 22%
        Gemstones: Trace
        Industrial Crystals: Trace
        Special Minerals: Trace
Cultural Data:
    Dominant Lifeform: Angelite
    Technological/Sociopolitical Index: 577763–77
    Planetary Trade Profile: BDHCBCA/D (D)

Typical Angelite

STR – 1D100		CHA – 1D100
END – 1D100		LUC – 1D100
INT – 1D100		PSI – 1D100
DEX – 1D100			

RACIAL DESCRIPTION

Female Angelites dominate the males, who are smaller and who fill the roles of homemaker and servant in the culture. Angelite women are sexist, and because they believe that the Federation oppresses women, the Angelites have refused to establish diplomatic relations with them.

Angelites are Human, with an average life expectancy of 78 years. The question of why the males born on the world are now smaller than the female has puzzled Federation scientists. Whether some environmental factor is the cause or whether it is the result of a cultural version of natural selection (small males are more attractive to the females and so they have a higher probability of mating) remains to be seen.

Angel One has a republican form of government ruled by an elected High Council, whose members are all female. Though the Angelites have been cut off from the Federation, they have made a large number of technological breakthroughs.

RELATIONS WITH THE FEDERATION

Angel One was rediscovered 58 years ago, but its leaders did not want anything to do with the Federation. During that time, the colony has had only a few visits from Federation starships. One civilian craft, the *Odin*, crashed on Angel One. Not bound by the Prime Directive, the survivors of the *Odin,* along with their Angel One wives, have become the center of a dissident movement attempting to change the sexist attitudes of the rest of the society.

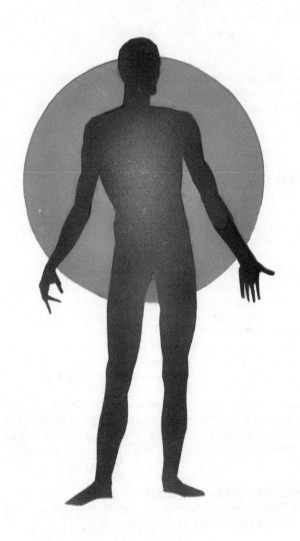

ANTICANS

World Log: ANTICA
System Data:
    System Name: Beta Renner
    Number of Class M Worlds: 2
Planetary Data:
    Position in System: 2
    Number of Satellites: 0
    Planetary Gravity: 1.0
    Planetary Size:
        Diameter: 18,000 km
        Equatorial Circumference: 56,500 km
        Total Surface Area: 1,017,876,000 sq km
        Percent Land Mass: 55%
        Total Land Area: 559,832,000 sq km
    Planetary Conditions:
        Length of Day: 20 hrs
        Atmospheric Density: Thick
        General Climate: Cool Temperate
    Mineral Content:
        Normal Metals: 38%
        Radioactives: 20%
        Gemstones: Trace
        Industrial Crystals: 09%
        Special Minerals: Trace
Cultural Data:
    Dominant Lifeform: Antican
    Technological/Sociopolitical Index: 564731–23
    Planetary Trade Profile: BFCDBHH/H(B)

Typical Antican

STR	50+3D10	CHA	1D100
END	50+3D10	LUC	1D100
INT	1D100	PSI	1D10+10
DEX	1D100		

RACIAL DESCRIPTION

Anticans are mammals that resemble large canines with large, elongated heads and who walk upright. They have long incisor teeth and sharp claws. Though they normally walk bipedally, they can run faster on all fours.

The average Antican has a life span of 50 years. Anticans mate often during their lives and remain with a mate only when children are small. A litter is anywhere from two to eight children, who are raised by the male.

Antican society is based on a pack concept. Anticans do not have true cities, but instead travel about as a kind of tribal pack. A central pack, with representatives from all of the others, is the closest thing to an Antican government. This body cannot make law and has no real power, but acts as an information clearing house.

Anticans live for the hunt and the ceremonial devouring of their kill. They do not eat fruits or vegetables or even frozen or simulated meats, preferring fresh raw meat.

Despite their nomadic life, Anticans have made several advances in weaponry, such as laser knives. Their sciences are fairly advanced, and Anticans seem to adapt to new technology quickly and effectively. They have never had a desire to travel in space until encountering the Selayans. Now they want to go into space to kill their sworn enemies.

RELATIONS WITH THE FEDERATION

From their earliest recorded history, the Anticans have been mobile in their pursuit of game. There are several small Antican cities, and these are the focal points for science and technology.

When the Selayans landed their crude spacecraft on Antica, they found the natives to be vicious and without mercy. An Antican hunting pack attacked the invaders, killing all but two of them and devouring their victims. The Selayans retaliated with several attacks that destroyed most of the pack, and the few survivors told the central pack of the new invaders.

The Anticans outnumber the Selayans, but do not have spaceflight technology or the weapons sophistication of their enemies. The Anticans believe that their home has been violated and that they, therefore, have the right to destroy every Selayan.

The Anticans view the Federation not so much as a mediator but as a potential ally against the Selayans. The Anticans believe that the Federation should help them destroy the Selayans and achieve space travel. The Antican central pack has heard rumors of the Ferengi but has no way to contact this government for help.

BINARS

World Log: BINAR
System Data:
    System Name: Beta Nirobi
    Number of Class M Worlds: 3
Planetary Data:
    Position in System: 3
    Number of Satellites: 0
Planetary Gravity: .79
Planetary Dimensions:
    Diameter: 9,650 km
    Equatorial Circumference: 30,300 km
    Total Surface Area: 292,553,000 sq km
    Percent Land Mass: 75%
    Total Land Area: 219,415,000 sq km
Planetary Conditions:
    Length of Day: 39 hours
    Atmospheric Density: Terrestrial
    General Climate: Warm Temperate
Mineral Content:
    Normal Metals: 58%
    Radioactives: 40%
    Gemstones: 10%
    Industrial Crystals: 08%
    Special Minerals: 02%
Cultural Data:
    Dominant Lifeform: Binar
    Technological/Sociopolitical Index: 998996–79
    Planetary Trade Profile: EDCCCDD/A (B)

Typical Binar:

STR	— 30+1D10	CHA	— 20+2D10
END	— 20+2D10	LUC	— 50+1D10
INT	— 50+2D10	PSI	— 1D10 –2
DEX	— 40+2D10		

RACIAL DESCRIPTION

The Binars are vaguely humanoid, short with pale gray-blue skin. They have no facial hair, and they speak quickly and precisely. They have large, quickly-moving eyes. There is little difference in the appearance of the males and females.

The Binars' only science is that of computer technology, for which they have no equals. Binar society is directly controlled by a global computer system. It appears that each Binar's life force is directly linked to the functioning of the master computer, regardless of the distance between the computer and the individual.

Binar language is, not surprisingly, a form of high-frequency coded transmissions in a mathematically based binary format that facilitates the rapid communications of massive amounts of information that each Binar receives and stores for "processing" as needed.

Binars always work in pairs and think only in terms of computers. When a Binar couple view the marvel of a *Galaxy* Class starship, for example, they think of it as nothing more than a large mobile computer. Binars answer any question with a "yes" or a "no," for they recognize no gray areas of thought.

RELATIONS WITH THE FEDERATION

The Binars have become so linked with their master computer that its growth and their destiny have become intertwined. They strive to learn all they can and to relay that information to the master computer. Their admittance to the Federation allows them to see and visit the galaxy, expanding their personal knowledge and thus also the data bank of their master system. If the master system shuts down, the Binars cease to function, and so they are very protective of it.

When a star near the Binar system went supernova, their Master System computer was threatened by the electromagnetic pulse that was generated. Recognizing the danger, a group of Binars used the pretext of updating the *USS Enterprise*'s computers to hijack the ship and take it to their system. Once there, the master computer loaded backup copies of all its data into the *USS Enterprise*'s massive system and then shut down just as the pulse passed the planet.

The information was restored to the system on Binar after the danger had passed. Though the Binars had, in effect, stolen the *Enterprise,* the crew found no damage and decided that the action was necessary for the Binars' self-preservation. The Federation Council has not pressed for sanctions, requesting only that the Binars ask for help from their allies in the future, instead of resorting to theft.

The Federation welcomes the arrival of the Binars. Their computer skills have provided many advances, both within and outside Starfleet. Many corporations have sent representatives to Binar to study their communication system for possible use in the Federation.

SELAYANS

World Log: SELAY
System Data:
    System Name: Beta Renner
    Number of Class M Worlds: 2
Planetary Data:
    Position in System: 1
    Number of Satellites: 1
Planetary Gravity: 1.0
Planetary Dimensions:
    Diameter: 15,600 km
    Equatorial Circumference: 49,000 km
    Total Surface Area: 764,538,000 sq km
    Percent Land Mass: 90%
    Total Land Area: 688,084,000 sq km
Planetary Conditions:
    Length of Day: 32 hours
    Atmospheric Density: Terrestrial
    General Climate: Desert
Mineral Content:
    Normal Metals: 40%
    Radioactives: 16%
    Gemstones: Trace
    Industrial Crystals: 03%
    Special Minerals: Trace
Cultural Data:
    Dominant Lifeform: Selayan
    Technological/Sociopolitical Index: 666662–45
    Planetary Trade Profile: FDEBFGH/D (D)

Typical Selayan

STR —	70 + 3D10	CHA —	20 + 3D10
END —	70 + 3D10	LUC —	1D100
INT —	1D100	PSI —	1D10
DEX —	20 + 3D10		

RACIAL DESCRIPTION

Selayans are large reptiles whose facial appearance is similar to a Terran cobra. They walk upright on two legs, and their two arms end in three-fingered hands with sharp, claw-like nails.

Selayans have a life span of approximately 110 years. They mate for life, and the female normally gives birth only once. She lays eggs, then protects them for five months, when the litter of up to eight offspring hatches. There are only about four million of this race.

Selayans have a strong dislike of mammals, particularly the vicious Hatcha Dogs that roam their world in packs. A Selayan traditionally wears long robes to conceal his weapon, which is usually a slug thrower. Gamemasters should treat this as a pistol.

RELATIONS WITH THE FEDERATION

The Selayans have been engaging in a bloody interplanetary war against the other sentient life form in their system, the Anticans.

A Federation mediator tried to establish diplomatic relations between the two worlds. Delegations from both sides are now meeting on the world of Parliament. Though a fragile cease-fire is in effect, for the most part, each side has just stated its grievances against the other with no attempt to seriously negotiate a final treaty. The Selayans are impatient, and they probably have established contacts with the Ferengi Empire in hopes of resolving their conflict more quickly.

BANDI

World Log: DENEB IV
System Data:
    System Name: Deneb
    Number of Class M Worlds: 1
Planetary Data:
    Position in System: 4
    Number of Satellites: 0
Planetary Gravity: 1.15
Planetary Dimensions:
    Diameter: 9,900 km
    Equatorial Circumference: 31,100 km
    Total Surface Area: 307,907,500 sq km
    Percent Land Mass: 90%
    Total Land Area: 277,117,000 sq km
Planetary Conditions:
    Length of Day: 32 hours
    Atmospheric Density: Terrestrial
    General Climate: Desert
Mineral Content:
    Normal Metals: 40%
    Radioactives: 22%
    Gemstones: 09%
    Industrial Crystals: 02%
    Special Minerals: Trace
Cultural Data:
    Dominant Lifeform: Bandi
    Technological/Sociopolitical Index: 888885–33
    Planetary Trade Profile: BBBCBDC/B (D)

Typical Bandi

STR	— 40+2D10	CHA	— 30+2D10
END	— 1D100	LUC	— 1D100
INT	— 1D100	PSI	— 1D10
DEX	— 1D100		

RACIAL DESCRIPTION

The Bandi are humanoids with a life expectancy of 80 years. They reach maturity at age ten. Most are light tan in color and wear their hair long.

These people are clan-oriented and closely tied to their geographical homelands. It is rare for a member of this race to move from one city to another, let alone to leave Deneb IV. A "Gropler" rules each tribe.

RELATIONS WITH THE FEDERATION

The Bandi recently informed the Federation that they had completed a star base for Federation use. The message strongly implied that the Ferengi Empire had also discovered the Bandi and had also made a bid for the new base. The Federation had just completed the *USS Enterprise,* and so Starfleet Command dispatched the new ship to investigate the base.

The base turned out to be a gigantic sentient lifeform that the Bandi were holding against its will. This space creature could manipulate matter, but it dropped onto Deneb IV when it began to run low on energy. It hoped to draw power from the geothermal energy under the surface. The Bandi helped the creature until they learned about its powers. Then the Bandi began to exploit the creature, giving it power only when it did as they said.

Another creature of the same kind destroyed much of the Bandi capital city and rescued the trapped one. The Bandi have since promised to build a new base for the Federation.

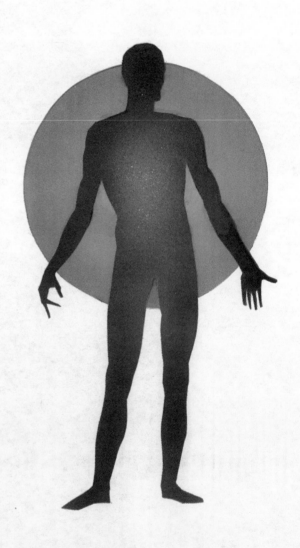

BETAZOIDS

World Log: BETAZED
System Data:
    System Name: Beta
    Number of Class M Worlds: 2
Planetary Data:
    Position in System: 2
    Number of Satellites: 0
    Planetary Gravity: .87
    Planetary Dimensions:
        Diameter: 9,500 km
        Equatorial Circumference: 29,800 km
        Total Surface Area: 283,529,000 sq km
        Percent Land Mass: 53%
        Total Land Area: 150,270,000 sq km
    Planetary Conditions:
        Length of Day: 18 hours
        Atmospheric Density: Terrestrial
        General Climate: Cool Temperate
    Mineral Content:
        Normal Metals: 45%
        Radioactives: 18%
        Gemstones: 10%
        Industrial Crystals: Trace
        Special Minerals: Trace
Cultural Data:
    Dominant Lifeform: Betazoid
    Technological/Sociopolitical Index: 889989–97
    Planetary Trade Profile: BBDDDDC/C (C)

Typical Betazoid

STR	— 35+3D10	CHA	— 60+3D10
END	— 30+3D10	LUC	— 1D100
INT	— 55+3D10	PSI	— 70+3D10
DEX	— 30+3D10		

RACIAL DESCRIPTION

Betazoids are statuesque humanoids who are very peaceful. There has not been a war or violent overthrow of a government on Betazed in recorded history, probably because of the nature of the race. Except for a typical life span of 100 to 150 years, Betazoids are physically similar to Humans, and there have been numerous unions between the two races.

Betazoids can read the emotions of most intelligent races. The range of this ability varies on the strength of the other person's feelings, but it is usually limited to the immediate vicinity. Betazoids communicate among themselves through telepathy, but will use verbal communication with races that do not have this power.

Not only can Betazoids read passive and directed emotional patterns, they can also read non-verbal expressions. By watching and listening to a person for a few moments, a Betazoid can determine if the person is withholding information or is being open and honest.

Betazoids are deeply tied to traditions and old values. A child is betrothed at an early age by the mutual consent of the parents. Such a marriage must take place before the female is 30 years of age, and most women marry in their late 20s.

RELATIONS WITH THE FEDERATION

The Betazoids' greatest impact on the Federation was the establishment of the position of Ship's Counselor within Starfleet. A Counselor assists command-rank officers by providing insight during First-Contact situations and during diplomatic negotiations. The Betazoids' ability to read emotions and intentions reduces the probability of hostilities when Starfleet makes First Contacts.

EDO

World Log: RUBICUN III
System Data:
    System Name: Rubicun
    Number of Class M Worlds: 1
Planetary Data:
    Position in System: 3
    Number of Satellites: 0
Planetary Gravity: .9
Planetary Dimensions:
    Diameter: 13,500 km
    Equatorial Circumference: 42,400 km
    Total Surface Area: 527,555,000 sq km
    Percent Land Mass: 40%
    Total Land Area: 229,022,000 sq km
Planetary Conditions:
    Length of Day: 20 hours
    Atmospheric Density: Terrestrial
    General Climate: Cool Temperate
Mineral Content:
    Normal Metals: 70%
    Radioactives: 10%
    Gemstones: Trace
    Industrial Crystals: Trace
    Special Minerals: Trace
Cultural Data:
    Dominant Lifeform: Edo
    Technological/Sociopolitical Index: 465443–50
    Planetary Trade Profile: AABBBBA/A (D)

Typical Edo

STR	70+3D10	CHA	70+3D10
END	70+3D10	LUC	1D100
INT	1D100	PSI	1D10
DEX	60+4D10		

RACIAL DESCRIPTION

The Edo are a beautiful humanoid race dedicated to good will and health. They welcome visitors with total hospitality and courtesy, sharing their facilities, food, and company.

Based on initial scannings of the planet's inhabitants, the Edo life expectancy is estimated at 92 years. Children have a high maturity level and are considered adults at the age of 12.

Edo society is based on health, with running and walking the accepted means of travel. There are no transporters on Rubicon III. The Edo wear tunics and togas. Their cities have vast open plazas surrounded by factories, spas, public pools, and restaurants. Though the Edo are highly advanced, there is little outward evidence of technology and no devices that cause pollution.

Rubicon's legal system must be dealt with carefully. Death is the punishment for any violation of the law. The Edo law enforcers randomly choose a new area for surveillance each day. If a violation occurs within this area, the enforcers arrive. They verify with witnesses that a violation has taken place. Then they give the violator a lethal injection; there is no plea bargaining or appeal.

This legal system keeps violations few and eliminates the need for a large police force or prison system. It also does not require a governmental body, reducing the political structure further.

The Edo are protected by a stellar entity they call "God." This entity exists in another dimension and can move freely between our universe and its own. This entity also enforces the laws. It will not allow the Edo to leave Rubicon, even if it means destroying a starship. Some Federation scientists believe that this entity placed the Edo on the planet as a long-term experiment to observe how the race would develop. This entity does sometimes take an active role in its people's lives.

RELATIONS WITH THE FEDERATION

The "God" entity has allowed the Federation to establish a colony nearby in the Strand system. Future contact with this entity is expected, and Federation and Starfleet personnel are urged to keep contact with the Edo at a minimum until more is known.

Federation experts believe that this entity is an extra-dimensional lifeform. Attempts at communications since the original encounter with the *USS Enterprise* have failed. This being can appear whenever it wishes, apparently from nowhere.

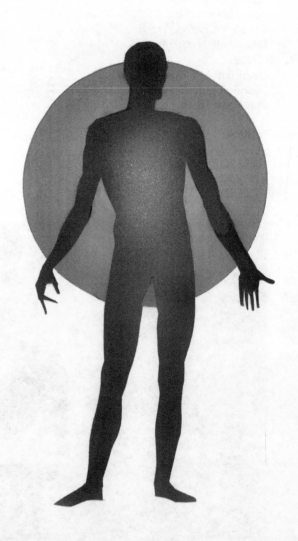

LIGONIANS

World Log: LIGON II
System Data:
    System Name: Ligon
    Number of Class M Worlds: 1
Planetary Data:
    Position in System: 2
    Number of Satellites: 0
Planetary Gravity: 1.1
Planetary Dimensions:
    Diameter: 16,000 km
    Equatorial Circumference: 50,200 km
    Total Surface Area: 804,248,000 sq km
    Percent Land Mass: 52%
    Total Land Area: 418,209,000 sq km
Planetary Conditions:
    Length of Day: 29 hours
    Atmospheric Density: Terrestrial
    General Climate: Warm Temperate
Mineral Content:
    Normal Metals: 30%
    Radioactives: 12%
    Gemstones: Trace
    Industrial Crystals: 08%
    Special Minerals: Trace
Cultural Data:
    Dominant Lifeform: Ligonian
    Technological/Sociopolitical Index: 576774–32
    Planetary Trade Profile: DFDDEEF/D (C)

Typical Ligonian

STR	60+3D10	CHA	1D100
END	40+3D10	LUC	1D100
INT	1D100	PSI	1D10
DEX	50+4D10		

RACIAL DESCRIPTION

Ligonians are dark-skinned humanoids who like to dress in bright colors. Leaders wear the skins of dead animals as a sign of power, but usually only at official functions and ceremonies. Males and females always wear a knife or other blade weapon, showing that they are a warlike race.

Their life expectancy is 94 years despite the harsh conditions on their planet. They are much like the Terran Zulu tribe in their actions and lifestyles, with a strict code of honor. Though the code of the warrior gives men greater status, women hold most of the property.

The government of Ligon is the all-male Tribal Council, which has representatives from the 39 tribes on the planet. Positions on the council are hereditary.

The law of Ligon is that of the challenge. If an article or point is contested, the two parties battle for it. Such contests are usually fought to the death using Berkas. A Berka is a large, mailed gauntlet covered with spikes. A dangerous poison tips each spike, causing death within moments if the point breaks the skin. Such fights are common public gatherings, with observers engaging heavily in wagers.

RELATIONS WITH THE FEDERATION

The Prime Directive has created some bitterness between the Federation and the Ligonians. The Ligonians want the benefits of Federation technology, and the Federation cannot tolerate death duels.

The Ligonians have used the technological advances they have made to develop processing of curative herbs and spices. The Ligonians also demand a high price for such remedies, hoping to pressure the Federation to relax cumbersome regulations and allow the Ligonians some new technology.

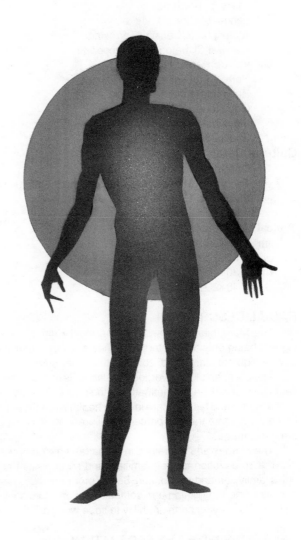

MORDANIANS

World Log: MORDAN IV
System Data:
    System Name: Idini Star Cluster
    Number of Class M Worlds: 1
Planetary Data:
    Position in System: 4
    Number of Satellites: 1
Planetary Gravity: 1.03
Planetary Dimensions:
    Diameter: 8,690 km
    Equatorial Circumference: 27,300 km
    Total Surface Area: 237,241,000 sq km
    Percent Land Mass: 32%
    Total Land Area: 75,917,000 sq km
Planetary Conditions:
    Length of Day: 18 hours
    Atmospheric Density: Terrestrial
    General Climate: Cool Temperate
Mineral Content:
    Normal Metals: 44%
    Radioactives: 30%
    Gemstones: Trace
    Industrial Crystals: 12%
    Special Minerals: 08%
Cultural Data:
    Dominant Lifeform: Mordanian
    Technological/Sociopolitical Index: 576950–44
    Planetary Trade Profile: HFFEEBC/B (C)

Typical Mordanians

STR	— 50+3D10	CHA	— 30+2D10
END	— 60+3D10	LUC	— 1D100
INT	— 30+2D10	PSI	— 1D10
DEX	— 40+2D10		

RACIAL DESCRIPTION

The Mordanians are shorter than most Humans, with the biggest being only two meters tall. They are very muscular and have a high pain threshold, compared to most Humans.

The life span of the average Mordanian is approximately 45 years because of the contamination of their world. The Mordanian Ambassador and his party are in better health since they left their homeworld. More than 35 percent of all pregnancies on Mordan are miscarriages.

The Mordanians are raised in a Spartan environment. They learn deep devotion to their families, and so any slight against one's family demands retribution. School programs include sports directly related to fighting and combat. Mordanians disdain protective gear, relying on their ability to cope with pain.

RELATIONS WITH THE FEDERATION

When the Federation encountered Mordan, its people were at a technological level equivalent to early 21st-century Terra, but ravaged by civil war. The Federation ambassador hoped to turn the Mordanians away from such destructive behavior.

Three years after the Federation opened trade relations with the Mordanians, Binak, one of the most important clan rulers, was assassinated. His son, Karnas, seized the passengers of a Federation luxury liner, demanding weapons to wipe out the clan responsible for his father's death.

After two Federation ambassadors were killed, Commander Mark Jameson took over the talks with Karnas. Jameson negotiated the release of the hostages, and the Federation quickly broke off relations with Mordan. Within a matter of months, the world erupted in a civil war that became the longest in Federation history, lasting 40 years and costing million of lives.

It was later discovered that Commander Jameson had given Karnas the phasers, as requested. In keeping with his interpretation of the Prime Directive, he gave comparable weapons to Karnak's rivals. Official Starfleet records still show, however, that Captain Jameson negotiated the release without giving in to Karnas's terms.

Mordan's relations with the Federation have been strained in the past 40 years, with the Mordanians believing that the Federation was responsible for their civil war. They recently took the Federation ambassador and her party hostage, demanding the return of now-Admiral Mark Jameson under the pretense of needing Jameson as a negotiator. With the death of Jameson on Mordan, the Mordanians consider that their grudge with the Federation is ended, and hope to establish normal relations.

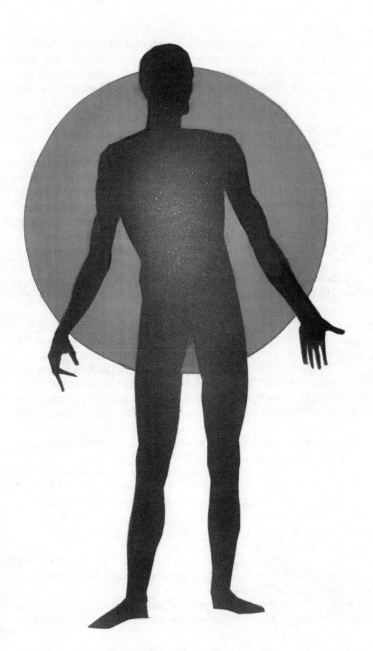

TURELLIANS

Typical Turellian

STR	— 50+3D10	CHA	— 1D100
END	— 1D100 −10	LUC	— 1D100
INT	— 1D100	PSI	— 1D100
DEX	— 1D100		

RACIAL DESCRIPTION

Turellians are a humanoid race who carry a dangerous infection that has decimated them. They still give birth, but only 10 percent of the children survive.

Turellians are a highly psionic people, though they do not utilize their powers to the extent that they could. They are drawn to other empathic or psionic races.

RELATIONS WITH THE FEDERATION

The tale of the Turellians is tragic. During a war between the inhabitants of the two major land masses on the planet, a bacteriological holocaust contaminated the ecosystem, and Turellians began to die by the millions. Those who fled into space found that they carried the plague with them. By the time the Federation began exploration, all of the Turellian colonies had been wiped out, leaving only a handful of survivors. These still carried the disease.

Nearly 100 Turellian starships roamed space searching for places to settle and perhaps even to find a cure. They brought death to the populations of several worlds. For a short time, several other races pursued the Turellian ships, destroying them rather than letting them travel freely and possibly pose a threat to others.

The last known encounter with the Turellians took place when a Turellian ship asked for permission to land at Haven. Through some difficult diplomacy, the ship was diverted from the system. Its last course was tracked by the *USS Enterprise,* and all Starfleet vessels are aware of the ship and its threat.

Starfleet personnel should note that there is no known cure for the plague that the Turellians carry. Personnel of the Federation are to offer aid to the Turellian ships but make no direct contact. Medical supplies or repair parts may be beamed to the Turellians, but they are considered to be under the strongest of quarantines.

Player characters who are exposed to the disease should make a Saving Roll against their END score with a - 50 modifier. If the roll is successful, they avoid contracting the disease, but are not immune. Every time they are exposed, the gamemaster should make the players repeat the Saving Roll.

Player characters who contract the disease take 5 points of wound damage at the start of each day, until death occurs. Since there is no known cure for the disease, an infected player character's only hope is that the disease will go into remission, i.e. stop the daily damage. Each day, the player should roll a 1D100. On a result of 100, the disease is in remission and the character stops taking damage, through his endurance is permanently reduced. Medical aid can help force the disease into remission. For every full 10 points of *General Medicine* skill, a doctor can lower the Remission Roll by 1 point. Characters who are in remission are still infectious.

FEDERATION ADVERSARIES LIST

In the years since the original *STAR TREK*, the political alignments have changed greatly. The Klingons are no longer the main enemy of the Federation, but an ally, yet there are still renegade Klingons who view the Federation with distaste. The Romulans, who disappeared from the scene for a period of years, have re-emerged as a major potential adversary.

And there are new threats, such as the Ferengi Empire and a little-known strain of parasitic insectoids. This section examines each of these potential adversaries of the Federation along with giving some gamemastering hints on how to incorporate characters of these races into a game plot.

RENEGADE KLINGONS

Racial Description

Gamemasters should use standard Klingon roleplaying statistics for Klingon characters.

Relations With the Federation

The treaty formally allying the Klingon Empire and the Federation has left some Klingons with a feeling of betrayal. Viewing the Klingons who have accepted the alliance as racial traitors, the renegade Klingons have been attempting, singly or in small groups, to leave known space and set up their own colonies in uncharted systems. Other renegade Klingons are attempting to sabotage the alliance from within.

The gamemaster should note that the majority of the Klingons have accepted the alliance with the Federation. The Klingon Defense Force (the old Imperial Klingon Navy) actively attempts to suppress the renegades. However, the gamemaster should also be aware of the potential for interesting game plots utilizing the conflict between the aggressive nature of the Klingons and their fidelity to their government.

THE FERENGI

Typical Ferengi

STR	— 50+4D10	CHA	— 3D10
END	— 1D100	LUC	— 1D100
INT	— 1D100	PSI	— 2D10
DEX	— 40+5D10		

Racial Description

A Ferengi has an enlarged cranium with little hair. Ferengis have large ears that meet over the eyes. They have sharp, uneven incisor teeth and are primarily meat-eaters. Though small, Ferengis are powerful and can move swiftly in a hunched, swaying motion.

In a fight, a Ferengi claws, kicks, punches, and bites in a frenzy. The Ferengi have no apparent code of honor or sense of fair play.

Profit appears to be the main Ferengi motivation, and wealth is a measure of status. Federation moral standards condemn most Ferengi behavior. A Ferengi would not only try to sell his own mother, he would also try to frame somebody else for doing it, turn in the buyer, and then split the profits with his mother, making sure that any witnesses never lived to tell the tale.

Little is known of the internal workings of the Ferengi culture. The highest rank encountered is that of "Daemon," which is believed to translate roughly as Merchant Prince. A small tattoo on the right forehead denotes rank. Ferengi women have little status. Females do not wear clothes.

History

The Federation learned of the Ferengi from several races that had encountered them, but these reports were sketchy.

The Federation encountered the Ferengi without knowing it. Several Starfleet vessels and independent trading ships fell victim to pirates of unknown origin. At first, the evidence pointed to a Romulan connection because these unknown ships destroyed themselves rather than allow capture. The physical evidence, however, pointed to a new race, one that matched the description of what the Federation knew of the Ferengi.

The first contact that was verified by the Ferengi Empire was an attack against the *USS Stargazer* in which both the Ferengi ship and the *Stargazer* were destroyed. This was confirmed only within the last year. Until that time, the Federation listed the *Stargazer* as lost in a battle against an unknown force.

Relations With the Federation

The Ferengi see the Federation as a great threat to their culture and race. They consider the Federation's Prime Directive as a ridiculous barrier to profit.

The Ferengi are not ignorant adversaries; they are cunning and deadly. They see the Federation as an enemy, but they want no direct confrontation.

The Ferengi have penetrated a wide area on the frontier of the Federation. Though the Klingon Defense Force has limited their penetration into the Klingon sphere of influence, Starfleet has only recently begun to address the Ferengi threat to peace. Increased patrols and protection of merchant ships from Ferengi pirating activities have become routine.

On at least one occasion, the Ferengi have tried to frame a well-known Starfleet Captain. Many suspect that they have a spy network that could extend to the Federation High Council. The Ferengi have a keen interest in Starfleet and its deployment on the frontier, which might indicate future activity on their part.

For the gamemaster, the Ferengi can be the simplest villain to use. Their ships are strong and their motivation is easy to game.

A little reading about 19th-century robber barons would probably help fill in their type. Remember, however, that the Fernegi are cunning and devious. Gamemasters should not present players with simple-minded scenarios, such as the Ferengi eliminating all native species on a planet so that they can seed it with profitable commercial animals. Ferengi plots should be much more complicated.

ROMULANS

Racial Description

Gamemasters should use standard Romulan roleplaying statistics for Romulan characters.

If the Klingons can be considered "brutish," the Rolumans should be considered "satanic." The Romulans have genetic links to the Vulcans, though the differences in personality seem to deny it. The Vulcans live by peace and logic; the Romulans are volatile and aggressive.

Romulans do not initiate combat but allow their opponent to start a fight. When dealing with Romulans, players should remember that a simple precaution such as raising shields can force the Romulans into an aggressive posture.

The new Romulan starships are impressive. They, too, have made improvements in their warp drive technology and their advancements in cloaking technology have kept pace with Federation sensors, making it just as difficult to find a cloaked ship as it was 80 years ago.

The Romulans broke contact with the Federation about five decades ago. They reappeared after the mysterious disappearance of several Federation listening outposts on the border with the Neutral Zone. A Romulan battlecruiser of the *Executioner* Class advanced across the Neutral Zone to establish contact with the *USS Enterprise*.

During this brief encounter, the Romulans revealed two interesting bits of information. They, too, had lost several outposts without warning. Second, they claimed to have been "occupied elsewhere" with a situation that has now been resolved.

Relations With the Federation

Within the past year, the Romulans have returned to the Neutral Zone with renewed interest in the Federation's growth. Several outposts reported cloaked vessels of unknown origin within sensor range. Though there is little doubt that these were Romulan ships, there is no proof of it. These incidents forced Starfleet to increase patrols along the Neutral Zone, reassigning ships from other details to make a show of force near Romulan space.

The Romulans and the Federation have agreed to an informal exchange of information on the loss of outposts.

Some Federation analysts believe that the Romulan Star Empire was expanding on its other borders and made contact with a hostile race. These analysts believe that the Romulans have resolved a long war with this enemy and are now turning their attention back to the Federation.

For gamemasters, the Romulans present a very good mixture of knowns and unknowns. Their history and racial characteristics can serve as a solid foundation of information for your players, while the events of the past 50 years lend the Romulans a sinister air that can be played upon well.

PARASITIC INVADERS

Typical Parasite

STR	– 2D10	CHA	– 1D10
END	– 1D10+5	LUC	– 2D10
INT	– 1D100	PSI	– 1D100
DEX	– 50+1D10		

Racial Description

This creature is a parasite 10 to 14 centimeters long and 4 centimeters wide. They have six legs, two antennae, and a 3-centimeter maw. The creature can breathe through its mouth or its tail. They are pale blue-gray and can move quite fast.

These insectoids enter a being through the mouth and head for the host's brain stem. Once there, they implant their antennae into the base of the brain to control all physical functions of the host. They also penetrate the neck of the victim to breathe with their tails. Entry of this lifeform into a host causes 1D10 damage. In attacking, the insectoid causes 1D10 + 1 with its maw.

Once in control of a body, the parasite can stimulate the adrenal glands to give the host fantastic strength (double normal STR and END Scores) and can even control the vocal cords. The creature does not enjoy humanoid foods, however, craving worms and larva. Also it cannot access the victim's long-term memory. Thus, by astute questioning, an alert player can discover if someone has been taken over (though the lifeform will attempt to evade such questioning).

A mother, or ruler creature, controls the other parasites and coordinates the actions of the insectoids. The destruction of this ruler, and unfortunately the host it is in, causes all the insectoids to retreat from their victims and to die shortly thereafter. Thus, these beings must be linked psionically. The destruction of one of these rulers foiled the race's plans for conquering the Federation.

History

This race entered the Federation by taking over an Away Team who were beamed back to the ship. The creatures rapidly took over the ship and headed back into known space.

From there, the lifeform spread through the Federation. The beings began to utilize their host bodies to control key commanders and positions within Starfleet. By attacking the Chief Medical Officer of a ship or a base so they could not be detected, the lifeform then took over the ship's Captain and First Officer. Eventually, the insectoids took control of the highest-ranking members in Starfleet Command. If it had not be for the fortuitous intervention of the *USS Enterprise,* the entire Federation would have fallen to these creatures.

Relations With the Federation

This race appeared to have been trying to gain control of the Federation, and they nearly succeeded. The insectoids took over the Command Staff at Starfleet Command and might have conquered the Federation were it not for the swift actions of William Riker and Jean-Luc Picard.

While the initial threat to Starfleet was stopped, gamemasters and players should not assume that the threat has been eliminated. Only one mother creature was destroyed. Other members of this species might still exist within the Federation borders. As a plot device, the parasitic lifeform allows the gamemaster to use well-established, friendly NPCs as integral parts of some devious plan.

In the years since the voyages of Captain James T. Kirk, Starfleet has undergone profound changes. The chain of command and shipboard duties have changed. New races have joined Starfleet, and the training of officers has changed. There are even new skills. The following rules and tables allow the gamemaster to incorporate these changes into **STAR TREK: The Role Playing Game.**

When creating a *Next Generation* character, the player should follow the normal pre- and post-academy procedures listed in the rule book. Only the Star Fleet Academy and Cadet Cruise sections are changed.

SHIPBOARD POSITIONS

The evolution of Starfleet over the past eight decades has demanded bridge officers who are more well-rounded individuals. Bridge positions were formerly staffed by an individual highly trained in a single area. Current Bridge personnel must now have several skills. Cross-training, or intermixing similar skills, gives Starfleet greater flexibility and provides personnel with background beyond a single area of expertise.

A classic example of this is the new position of Bridge Command Specialist. In the past when a Helmsman was injured, a replacement was called to the Bridge, wasting time. Now a pair of Bridge Command Specialists can perform each other's duties. If a Helmsman falls in combat, the Navigator can assume Helm duties until a backup arrives. The same is true for the Tactical Officer, who is trained to operate the starship's weapons as well as its security systems.

This removes some of the burden of role separation inherent in the STRPG. Because so many key officers have training in a variety of systems, players can try new roles and duties on the Bridge without transferring to new career path or school.

Following are descriptions of the new roles available during *The Next Generation.*

BRIDGE COMMAND SPECIALIST

Two of these individuals are on the Bridge at all times, with at least two others on standby. These officers are trained in both Helm and Navigation, and one assumes each of these duties. A Bridge Command Specialist is also trained in Communications and can control hailing frequencies, though the Security Specialist normally handles this function. The two control panels are identical. Thus, each Bridge Command Specialist can assume all controls and duties if the other individual is incapacitated or the other control panel is inoperative.

Because of the close interaction, Bridge Command Specialists train together and often work together throughout their careers. A specialist in this area emerges from Starfleet Academy with the following skills.

BRIDGE COMMAND SPECIALIST SKILLS

Astrogation	10
Communication Systems Operation	20
Computer Operation	20
Deflector Shield Operation	20
Navigation/Helm	30
Negotiations/Diplomacy	20
Sensor Analysis	10
Starship Combat Strategy/Tactics	10
Starship Helm Operation	40

SECURITY SPECIALIST

Security Specialist is in charge of starship security, both internal and external. This person controls the ship's alert status, intership communications, and shield operation, relieving the Bridge Command Specialists. The Security Specialist also controls all weapons in combat. A Security Specialist emerges from Starfleet Academy with the following skills.

SECURITY SPECIALIST SKILLS

Communication Systems Operation	30
Communication Systems Technology	10
Computer Operation	20
Damage Control Procedures	30
Deflector Shield Operation	20
Deflector Shield Technology	10
Electronics Technology	20
Marksmanship, Modern	10
Personal Combat	
Armed	10
Unarmed	10
Security Procedures	40
Small Equipment Systems Operation	20
Starship Combat Strategy/Tactics	20
Starship Weaponry Operation	20

SCIENCE SPECIALIST

This position has evolved over the past 80 years. This officer is in charge of sensor operations and analysis and maintaining the ship's life-support systems. The Life Science Specialist commands the Science Station on the Bridge. An officer with this specialty emerges from Starfleet Academy with the following skills.

SCIENCE SPECIALIST

Computer Operation	40
Life Sciences	3 at 10 Each
Life Support Systems Technology	20
Medical Sciences	
General Medicine (Choose Race)	30
Psychology (Choose Race)	20
Other	(1 at 10)
Sensor Analysis	30
Space Sciences	2 at 10 Each
Starship Sensors	30
Other Skills	Total of 40 points

ENGINEERING SYSTEMS SPECIALIST

The role of the Engineering Officer is essentially the same as in the past, except that this specialist now needs some knowledge of the helm and navigation systems. The cross-training of the Engineering Systems Specialist is also much broader, taking new technology into account.

ENGINEERING SYSTEMS SPECIALIST

Communication Systems Technology	10
Computer Operation	40
Computer Technology	10
Electronics Technology	20
Holodeck Systems Technology	10
Life Support Systems Technology	10
Mechanical Engineering	30
Navigation/Helm	20
Physical Sciences	
Physics	20
Space Sciences	
Astronautics	10
Starship Helm Operation	20
Starship Weaponry Technology	10
Transporter Systems Technology	10
Warp Drive Technology	20

Three of the above skills may be raised to 20, or 30 points may be added in new skills.

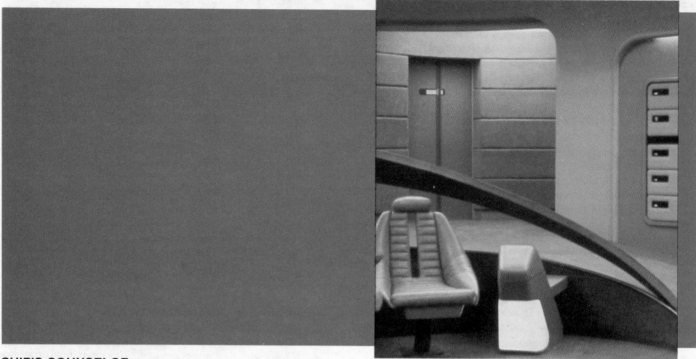

SHIP'S COUNSELOR

A new role in Starfleet, the Ship's Counselor position is always manned by a member of a telepathic race, primarily Betazoids, though several other races, such as Deltans, could fill this position. The Ship's Counselor evaluates the crew's mental and emotional conditions and establishes contacts with new races. The Ship's Counselor often works with the Chief Medical Officer to maintain morale aboard a starship.

A Ship's Counselor has undeniable access to meetings and events aboard a starship and takes part in all diplomatic and Away Team missions. A Ship's Counselor graduates from Starfleet Academy with the following skills.

SHIP'S COUNSELOR

Computer Operation	10
Communication Systems Operation	20
Communication Systems Technology	10
Languages	4 at 20 Each
Medical Sciences	
Psychology	Any 3 Races at 20 Each
Negotiations/Diplomacy	30
Social Sciences	3 at 15 Each
Starship Sensors	20
Transporter Operation Procedures	10

CADET CRUISE TABLE

10 or less	Exploration Command (*Galaxy* Class)
11–45	Exploration Command
46–75	Colonization Command
76+	Terraforming Command

In all other areas of character generation where benefits were awarded for service on *Constitution* Class ships in the original game, this now applies only to *Galaxy* Class starships.

TERRAFORMING COMMAND

This function was provided by Colonization Command, but the vast efforts and manpower needed led Starfleet to create a separate branch 43 years ago.

The Terraforming Command takes worlds that are not Class M and makes them habitable. This process can take 30 to 50 standard years, and only now is the Federation beginning to reap benefits from worlds where terraforming was originally done.

The Colonization Command searches for non-Class M worlds that are free of life or the prospect of developing life. These worlds must meet a stringent set of criteria for development.

The Terraforming Command then takes over, introducing atmosphere and water and controlling the climate. Technicians carefully construct a biosphere, with plant and animal life in perfect balance. When the Terraforming Command is finished, it turns the world over to Colonization Command for populating with humans.

This branch has only a few science vessels and stations and limited personnel.

Because the Terraforming Command and Colonization Command have some duplication of tasks and duties, they can be equated for purposes of character generation.

OTHER SPECIALISTS

Though STRPG deals extensively with graduates of Starfleet Academy, Starfleet also has personnel who have received very intensive training in one specific technical area. Unlike the integrated training program at Starfleet Academy, Specialists receive education in their primary skill areas only.

Individuals qualified for shipboard service receive three years of rigid supervision at the Starfleet Specialist School on Deneva. During the first year of training, personnel undergo a tough regimen of physical and psychological conditioning in preparation for shipboard duties, including familiarization with standard Federation equipment. During the second year, the recruit receives advanced training at a Specialist Center.

The list of pre-Academy skills is identical to those listed in STRPG. Selection of these skills is based on the same criteria as well.

BASIC CURRICULUM

A Specialist character uses the Basic Curriculum instead of the Academic Curriculum. Starfleet Basic Curriculum recruits receive the following Skills:

Computer Operation	15
Environmental Suit Operations	20
Federation Law	10
Marksmanship	20
Personal Combat	
Armed	25
Unarmed	20
Planetary Survival	20
Small Equipment Systems Operation	20
Transporter Operation Procedures	10
Zero-G Operations	20

OUTSIDE ELECTIVES

Following are electives available to the individual during the Starfleet Basic Curriculum course. The player must choose five electives from the list at a rating of 10 points each.

Artistic Expression
Carousing
Gaming
Marksmanship, Archaic
Sports
Streetwise
Trivia

Though Starfleet Academy candidates enter one of several branch schools, Specialist recruits have a choice of only three areas of specialization: Engineering, Sciences, and Medicine.

ENGINEERING SPECIALIZATION TRAINING SKILLS

Computer Operation	20
Computer Technology	15
Damage Control Procedures	15
Electronics Technology	10
Mechanical Engineering	10

30 points in any one of the following areas or 10 points extra in any of the above areas:

Communication Systems Technology
Deflector Shield Technology
Holodeck Systems Technology
Personal Weapons Technology
Ship's Engineering
Small Equipment Systems Technology
Starship Weaponry Technology
Transporter Systems Technology
Warp Drive Technology

MEDICINE SPECIALIZATION TRAINING SKILLS

Botany	10
Life Support Systems Technology	10
Negotiations/Diplomacy	10
Starship Sensors	15
Zoology	10

30 points in any one of the following areas or 10 points extra in any of the above areas:

General Medicine (up to three races)
Psychology

SCIENCE SPECIALIZATION TRAINING SKILLS

Astronomy/ Astrophysics	20
Computer Operation	20
Planetary Ecology	15
Starship Sensors	15

30 points in any one of the following areas or 10 points extra in any of the above areas:

Botany
Archeology
Chemistry
Geology

Graduates have the rank of Specialist. As player characters, specialists have 1D10 tours of duty prior to beginning their position in the game.

They should roll once on the Tour of Duty Table for each tour of duty using the standard die modifiers for INT and LUC.

TOUR OF DUTY TABLE

01–25	Exploration Command (Starship Duty)
26-50	Exploration Command (Starbase Duty)
51–55	ColonizationCommand (Starship Duty)
56-75	Colonization Command (Starbase Duty)
76+	Terraforming Command (Starbase Duty)

Specialists use the same modifiers table as listed in the STRPG.

Service skill rolls for Specialists are as per the rules listed in the STRPG.

OTHER CHANGES

The changing nature of Starfleet alters roleplaying in even more ways. There are new skills and new procedures. Some of these are examined here.

NEW CHARACTER SKILLS

Holodeck Operations Procedure

This skill is the ability to program simple instructions into the holodeck and to alter existing programs. The higher the level of skill, the more complicated the program that the player can create. Instructors, especially those at the Academy, have a high rating in this area because they use the holodeck as a training tool.

Holodeck Systems Technology

This skill relates to the technical aspects of the holodeck. An individual with this skill background can perform emergency rescue operations on a holodeck that is running a program. He can also halt a program without harming the people who are using the holodeck. This skill relates closely to *Transporter Systems Technology* because the same principles operate both devices.

AWAY TEAM

Fifty years ago, Starfleet implemented standards for assembling an Away Team or landing party. The purpose of the Away Team is to conduct scientific and cultural research away from the ship and/or to conduct diplomatic missions that the ship's Captain deems necessary.

The modern-day Away Team differs from its predecessors in that it is intended to minimize risk to a ship's Captain. Starfleet Command was concerned over the unnecessary risks often taken by command officers as members of landing parties because they could lead to the loss of experienced, highly trained, and valuable senior officers in situations that might be handled by subordinates. Current Starfleet regulations forbid a ship's Captain to undertake command of an Away Team (though he or she may subsequently join the team if circumstances warrant and the Away Team's commanding officer agrees).

The gamemaster should keep this restriction in mind when creating characters. If a group primarily engages in off-ship adventures, then the person who is playing the captain will end up having very little to do during the session. It might be advantageous for the group to have the ship's Captain be a nonplayer character.

WEAPONS CHART

WeaponType	Damage	Point Blank	Short	Range Medium	Long	Extreme	Power	Graze	Drain	Overload Radius
Hand Phaser	-	1	2-13	14-40	41-75	76-120	80			130 squares
Stun	80							30*	1	
Wide-angle stun	80*							30*	3	
Heavy stun	140*							80*	4	
Heat	50							25	1	
Disrupt	170							75	2	
Disintegrate	destroyed							70	4	
Pistol Phaser		1	2-17	18-50	51-80	81-130	90			150 squares
Stun	80*							30*	1	
Wide-angle stun	80*							30*	3	
Heavy stun	140*							80*	4	
Heat	60							30	1	
Disrupt	180							80	3	
Disintegrate	destroyed							75	4	
Ferengi Whip		1	2-12	13-35	36-68	69-110	45			100 squares
Heavy Stun	140*							140*	3	
Disrupt	175							75	2	
Disintegrate	destroyed							80	5	